THE CLOUD FACTORY

ALSO BY LAURIE OTIS

NOVELS

The Amarantha Stories

THE CLOUD FACTORY

STORIES & POEMS BY

WISCONSIN AUTHOR

LAURIE OTIS

Dianna,
My roommate
& friend
Laurie

Little Big Bay LLC

LITTLE PLACE ~ BIG IDEAS ~ ON THE BAY

www.littlebigbay.com

THE CLOUD FACTORY

Author: Laurie Otis

Cover pastel art: Laurie Otis

Illustrator: Jan MacFarlane

Book editor & designer: Roslyn Nelson

Printed in the United States of America

ISBN: 978-0-9834330-5-7
Library of Congress Control Number: 2012936342

Publisher: Little Big Bay LLC
littlebigbay.com

DEDICATED TO

ALL MY FRIENDS

IN WASHBURN, WISCONSIN

FOR THEIR

LOVE AND SUPPORT

TABLE OF CONTENTS

The cloud factory

The question is not what you look
at but what you see.

Henry David Thoreau

Dear Reader,

A friend told me the story of when she and her two children moved to Ashland, Wisconsin, the old hometown. Rather than a happy homecoming, it was an economic necessity in the wake of a devastating divorce; her parents would help until the family could regroup. She was trying desperately to view the move as a new, happy beginning but was constantly assailed by memories of betrayal and deceit, to say nothing of owning a personal measure of regret and failure.

They entered Ashland via the scenic Lake Shore Drive and just as she was thinking how beautiful and majestic Lake Superior was, they rounded a crest in the road and saw the institutional power company building, perched at water's edge, its huge chimney belching clouds of dark vapor into the clear, blue sky. Her fragile mood immediately turned as she inwardly raged, "Does everything have to be spoiled?" Then, in that same split second, her daughter jumped excitedly to the window and shouted in a voice so filled with delight and wonder that it could only come from a child,

"Oh look, Mom! Ashland has a cloud factory!"

I've thought of that story many times over the years, not only because of its obvious life lesson, but because I'm a cloud watcher. Oh, not for predicting the weather, although that can be very helpful at times. Being a dreamer I tend to spend some outdoor time studying shapes in the sky and, if I'm feeling particularly imaginative, I can't help but see animals or people. It's all fleeting, because the vapor disperses so quickly.

I love the big, fluffy cumulous clouds that on a summer's day float and mound themselves into castles and mountains. Somehow, I also love it when they suddenly form thunderheads and turn black with rain and lightning. I love the streaks of cirrus clouds that run scudding before the wind in their never-ending race. All types of clouds are alternately beautiful, ugly, solid, fleeting, safe, dangerous; and don't forget, appearances change with the eyes of every beholder – another metaphor for life!

So when it came time to name this book, I tried to think of something besides the boring, *My Short Stories* or a cutesy, *This & That*. What did these stories have in common? Each was a commentary on life. Each depicted inevitable change. Each suggested that the reader form an opinion. They are illusional, changing and open to interpretation, like dreams or visions or... clouds. Then I remembered my friend's story and thought *The Cloud Factory* would be the perfect name for this offering.

I hope you enjoy your venture into the wild, blue yonder.

– Laurie Otis

On finding a new home

When I was in elementary school, a long time ago, our teacher announced a new motivational competition. Whoever maintained the highest grades for five consecutive days would earn 15 minutes of extra recess. It was a brutal race. Tempers flared, tears fell, and friendships were sorely tested. Somehow (I think because Bobby Shafer was home with the mumps and Mary Stern threw up during a test) I emerged the winner. It was a sweet victory. The teacher wrote my name in her best calligraphy on the board, and recess that day was a triumph. The girls gathered around me in jealous admiration and the boys called out things like, "lucky stiff" and "must be nice." Even the bullies who called me egghead and teacher's pet couldn't penetrate that aura of specialness that encompassed me like a bubble. Then the bubble burst with the ringing of the bell heralding the end of recess. My classmates all filed into the building, my friends casting envious looks back at me, as I sat alone on a swing in a deserted playground. Winning isn't everything!

After 65 years, this episode popped into my mind when I'd been retired for about a month. I discovered that most of my friends were work related and younger, and even though I lingered over the crossword puzzle, consumed endless cups of coffee, and took walks in the woods, the days got long when there was nowhere to go, nothing to do, and nobody to go with me. I was right back on that swing, and alone.

Now, I had always thought of Ashland, Wisconsin as my hometown. I'd worked there for 30 years, was a Northland College graduate, had married into a local family, and kept Ashland ties even after moving to my present home about five miles north of Washburn, only 30 minutes from Ashland but a new town nonetheless. Putting in a nine-to-five work day had left little time for exploring my new community or volunteering for civic events, so pretty much all I knew of Washburn was what I observed on my daily drive down its long main street on my way home.

I noticed the renovations at the historic bank building and watched the addition rise and blend into the old landmark as if it had always been there. Then, as I drove by one dark November evening, I noticed that strings of white lights framed every window. The old building had been reborn and seemed to be announcing that it was ready for service. For me it seemed to announce that it was time to find a new hometown.

That was how, upon retirement, I came to volunteer at the Washburn Historical Society and Cultural Center. It was a difficult initiation, as Christmas was upon us, and there were two huge rooms to decorate in preparation for the big holiday concert, public reception, visit from Santa, and sleigh ride. It was overwhelming!

I was one of a group of Washburn ladies who volunteered to haul the sorriest collection of artificial trees (permanent lights burned-out, bare and rusty wire where artificial needles had worn away, unbelievably dusty) up from the basement, shake them off, rewind them with new lights, and twist their rusty branches (risking the need for tetanus shots) into a semblance of the traditional Tannenbaum.

A collection of huge, artificial mice presented another problem. Salvaged from some department store's animated Christmas display, these anthropomorphized specimens no longer possessed working mechanisms and were dusty, disheveled, and torn. But we wrestled them into the elevator and sewed, patched, and perked them up as best we could. Several times I suggested, "Why don't we just scrap it all and start anew?" To which our leader would reply, "We don't have a budget for this. It'll be fine!"

The night of the festivities arrived. We had baked cookies, made punch, set a glowing table, and stood in our best Yuletide finery in wait for the populace of Washburn to arrive. And arrive they did! Hundreds of people came to hear the *Boys' Choir*; the local high school show choir *Fire & Ice*; The *Harmony Studio Violinists*; the carolers; and storytellers. The guests enjoyed a delicious variety of hors d'oeuvres donated by Washburn businesses; and the children took home a memory of not only talking to Mr. and

Mrs. Santa, but a sleigh ride on a vintage farm sled drawn by a team of horses. In the midst of all the revelry, I stood back and took a good look around. The trees sparkled as if in a snow-laden forest. Tots approached the reconstructed mice in awe, touching their paws and adjusting the bonnets on the girl mice and the straw hats on the boy mice. *We had truly worked some kind of magic*, I thought, because it looked wonderful! Then again, maybe it wasn't us at all, but that old building itself that worked the alchemy!

And so, that was the The Friends of the Museum as I knew it. With an ever-changing group of women, we went on to decorate for holidays; bake; serve Christmas boutique lunches; edit a hometown cookbook; organize a brownstone tour; make and sell corn husk dolls; and host many receptions. I consider the people I have met at the Cultural Center to be my very good friends and look back on the events I've worked on as enjoyable memories. And these connections (nowadays they call it networking) have opened up even more activities for me.

I look forward every Thursday morning to painting with The Brownstone School, which has been meeting at the Cultural Center for about six years. To extend the network, The Brownstone School inspired the formation of a cooperative where many of its original members operate the Superior Artists' Gallery.

An so, one thing leads to another. One rock dropped into Lake Superior will produce several drops of water which, in turn, form intersecting circles. The Washburn Cultural

Center has truly become that rock on Lake Superior that is a center for the town, and even though many of us can't boast that we are native sons or daughters, we can adopt a new hometown by becoming involved.

P.S. I'm not alone on the playground any more. For many years now, I've been sharing the swing with lots of new friends.

All roads lead home

Home is the sailor, home from the sea,
And the hunter home from the hill.

Robert Louis Stevenson

This story begins with an excerpt from one of Clayton Videen's favorite poems.

Geneva and Clayton Videen moved to Washburn, Wisconsin in 1993; both were 83 years old. For Geneva it was a homecoming, since she had been born here, while Clayton had been born in Kingsdale, Minnesota. They had lived happily and prosperously for over fifty years in San Francisco, California, but came home when they found themselves increasingly alone in the big city; their health began to fail; and they realized they needed their extended family. Wherever they were, they had always embraced life with great enthusiasm and continued to do so after they moved to Washburn, concerning themselves with the Cultural Center, the Library, and family activities.

Eventually, Geneva could no longer care for Clayton, now blind, and he became a resident of the Northern Lights Nursing Home. Geneva lived in the assisted living apartments close by and visited him faithfully every day. Clayton died in April of 2004 at the age of 92. After seeing her husband of over 60 years laid to rest, Geneva followed close behind in December of 2004 also at the age of 92, her life's work being done.

When their estate was settled, the extent of their regard for Washburn became evident by bequests made to various community institutions. It was deemed that the $50,000 contribution to the Cultural Center roof fund deserved an article in the spring newsletter and prompted an interview with Jerry Doucette, Geneva's baby brother and longtime resident of Washburn. As we talked, Jerry mentioned that Clayton had written a book and offered to let me read it.

I must admit I looked rather balefully at the thick, spiral-bound tome he gave me. The cover read, *The Hard Life and Good Times of Clayton A. Videen by Himself*, and I imagined a boring genealogy. But I quickly changed my mind when I began reading what proved to be a fascinating chronicle of two members of the greatest generation, spanning a period of time from World War I, the great depression, World War II, and on through the eighties. Although the book is mainly Clayton's reminiscences of childhood, friends, jobs, hobbies, and family, interspersed in it is a firsthand account of American and world history as it happened, enhanced by popular song and movie titles, current book titles, beloved poetry, and his own wry political commentary. "The government hasn't learned what almost every adult with an eighth grade education knows. You can't continue to spend more than you take in..." is one of many comments made prophetic by the clarity of hindsight. He describes his literary effort as a result of, "...thousands of pages of diaries that go back to 1927, and carbon copies of thousands of letters dating back to 1936."

Of course, all good books have a love story, and this is no exception, not to mention essential for the Washburn connection. Fate brought Geneva and Clayton to Duluth and the mysterious hand of fate also prompted them to both move to a rooming house across from Central High School.

Young Clayton, by his own admission (and maybe a little boasting) was quite the ladies' man. He'd had many girlfriends, been in love several times, and had his heart broken at least once. So this experienced young man was taken aback when Geneva, "was polite to me, as if to tolerate me, but that was all." It was then he really became interested in this sad, quiet, country girl from Washburn. "She was tall, dark haired and had very large brown eyes. She conducted herself like a real lady and I liked that." And so the talking grew to dating, going steady, and finally marriage in 1942.

They decided that their future together lay in California and embarked on the long, cross-country trip by train. They first made a goodbye stopover in Washburn. Clayton remembered Geneva's father who felt his daughter was going to never-never land and that he wouldn't see her again. "His eyes filled with tears, and he pulled his hat down over his eyes and stalked away."

No, *Hard Life and Good Times* doesn't read like an Oprah best seller, but it has some pretty incredible true stories. If I hadn't read the book, I would not have known that Clayton and his brother rode the rails from Minnesota to California during the economic depression of the '30s, hitching rides in box cars and working odd jobs to make a living.

I wouldn't have known that Geneva, the oldest of nine born in Washburn to Hattie and William Doucette, had been widowed at 18 when her first husband, Floyd Hudson, was killed in a construction accident while working on County Road C outside of Washburn. Starting a new life, she worked to put herself through Duluth Business College and secure a career that would take her from clerking at various businesses, to working as a private secretary, to finally managing the entire audio-visual department for the San Francisco School Board.

I wouldn't have known that Clayton and his brother signed on a Swedish freighter that traveled to Japan, doing all sorts of menial, swabbie's jobs. His stories of the sea voyage, crew members, and happenings aboard ship are topped only by his description of Yokohama and the Japanese people.

"It is difficult to comprehend their dedicated brutality in the Second World War. But, jingoistic nationalism is capable of a great deal, especially in such a disciplined society," concluded Clayton.

I wouldn't have known that the boy from Kingsdale who was, "brought up in poverty and grew up on salt pork, boiled or fried potatoes and oatmeal," would some day own a company that designed air conditioning for large business buildings throughout California.

Their lives were truly adventurous, exciting, and rewarding, and I consider myself lucky to have come to know them, even if it was only through the pages of Clayton's book and by accident at that. Their gift to the Washburn Cultural Center will remind us that "the little town on the big lake" had always lain softly on their memories during all the years in San Francisco. The Videens' long and captivating journey of life began and ended in Washburn, proving once again the age-old adage, "All roads, physical or spiritual, lead home."

The cowboy boots

A remembrance of my salad days,
when I was green in judgment.

Shakespeare

One day, cleaning a closet suddenly became a trip down memory lane.

Stacked against the back wall were shoe boxes that often toppled when the door was opened, depositing their contents across the closet floor. Then came my task of sorting and placing them back into spaces made to fit only if the shoes were laboriously arranged heel to toe and placed on their sides flat to the bottom of the box. The lids, of course, hadn't closed properly since that first exciting moment when I'd carelessly pried them off, eager with the anticipation of viewing again the treasures I'd found – and on sale! Time for a trip to the thrift shop, but not before I had one last look.

Ah, the blue suede shoes, rescued from the bottom of a closeout bin because I was stricken with a fit of nostalgia and still, after all these years, secretly in love with Elvis. They're just like new!

Next came the earth shoes designed for the utmost in foot health but also, unfortunately, the utmost in ugly (they're the forerunner of Crocs™). What can I say when in the '60s, even the newly liberated, free-love feminists, who burned their bras and quit shaving their armpits and legs, wouldn't be caught dead wearing them?

So went the parade of shoes deemed unsuitable for various reasons: the espadrilles that took at least a half hour and total concentration to lace; Dr. Scholl's® sandals with a bed-of-nails sole that rendered you crippled for two days after wearing them.

Then what should turn up, there at the bottom of the stack, well worn and scuffed, but my trusty, old cowboy boots! I'd forgotten all about them. Oh, they weren't the tall kind; my ample calves could never accommodate that style. No, they were ankle length and devoid of any gaudy coloring or skillful tooling; but their slanted heels and pointed toes could still fit a stirrup and suggested the historical and much glorified mystery of the Old West which lurks so romantically in our American psyches.

I remember the day I bought these, I mused as I held one shoe lovingly in my hand and turned it absentmindedly. A colleague and I had been driving north from a business meeting and stopped in a small town along our route for a cold drink. As we walked from the restaurant we passed a shoe store window, and there they were, turned provocatively, as if inviting each other to launch into a two-step. Now, I am normally a very conservative dresser, but there was something about those boots that spoke to me of breaking the mold, abandoned fun, and loving life.

"What do you think?" I said, as I viewed their reflection in the mirror, turning and stepping back and forth in mimicked stances.

"They look great," my friend answered, distracted by trying to negotiate complicated straps on a pair of sandals.

"They're not too far out, but they're a little more daring than I usually buy, they're just right," I concluded, applying the Goldilocks method of decision making. Of course they cried out for a pair of stove-pipe legged jeans and a denim shirt, which I purchased in the next store, causing me to be wracked with my Scandinavian self-imposed guilt for the rest of the ride home.

I put the whole outfit together the next Saturday night and stood at the full-length mirror. I hooked my thumbs in the belt loops and bent one knee. I turned my profile and made a gun of my thumb and forefinger. I sat down on the edge of my bed, rested my elbows on my knees and looked at my new boots. "What was I thinking?" I said aloud to the dog who had been watching my antics. Then a car horn sounded. My girl friends and I were going to Club 13 for a night of the newest craze, line dancing.

"It's great," a girl at the bar assured us, "You don't have

to wait around all night for some guy to ask you to dance. You don't need a partner. You don't need no stinkin' men!" The latter was delivered loudly with her drink raised in a toast, causing several stinkin' men to look our way, shaking their heads. There went any hope of a partner for a tender ballad.

Then we all trooped onto the dance floor together and lined up in rows. Our teacher stood in front and briefly demonstrated the basic steps before the music swelled, and we all haltingly stepped backwards, forwards, sideways, turned around, and repeated, bumping into each other and getting tangled in our own feet. We were weak with laughter and leaned on each other to get our breath. It was a tough workout and we were forced to drink beer during the breaks just to keep hydrated; our teacher, who was also the bar owner, cautioned us that this was very important.

"I got friends in low places," Garth Brooks sang again and again into the night as we perfected the choreography by repetition. It was the most fun I'd had in years! Even a few of the stinkin' men joined us. It was the first of many such nights at Club 13, now, alas, razed and gone.

"I was in the loop then, working, productive, relevant," I thought. That was so many years ago. And the reverie continued.

These old boots were handy by the door when I received the call and rushed to the hospital to view the birth of my first grandson. The boots trudged with me to hide Easter eggs for the hunt; they crawled under the tree to arrange presents; they were there when we went as a group to raise our glasses in one last hurrah to a fallen sister line dancer taken, sadly, before her time.

I shrugged off my fleece slipper and tried to cram my foot into the stiff boot; but several extra pounds and years of wearing nothing but Nike and Birkenstock® shoes had taken their toll; the cowboy boots no longer fit. The life they represented no longer fit either, I admitted to myself.

Now my friends and I get together for coffee, or painting, or watching movies. No one likes to drive after dark any more so the odd night out to a movie in Ashland and a sandwich at the 2nd Street Bistro is treated as a real fling, with someone always observing, "Look at us, out on a Saturday night!" The most difficult part is when we raise our glasses in one last hurrah to a fallen sister taken, sadly, in a timely fashion.

I ease my foot back into my slipper and snuggle into the unrestricted comfort. *My foot doesn't have to fit into the stirrup any more,* I muse. My friends and I are truly relevant to each other, and it's really nice to just float, occasionally treading water. I sit looking at the boots a few seconds longer, when suddenly it comes to me. I think I'll have them bronzed.

Growing pumpkins
(Cucurbitaceae)

*One day I found two pumpkin seeds. I planted one and pulled
the weeds. It sprouted roots and a big, long vine.*

*A pumpkin grew; I called it mine. The pumpkin was quite round
and fat (I really am quite proud of that.)*

*But there is something, I'll admit, that has me worried just a bit.
I ate the other seed, you see.*

Now will it grow inside of me?*

Anonymous poet **See end of story for answer.*

What is more rewarding for a gardener than growing pumpkins, squash, or gourds, all of the family cucurbitaceae? The plants are easy to grow; they are prolific and often grow impressive specimens of fruit, depending on the type of seed variety.

This is strictly an informational piece on growing the fruit. Yes, I said fruit, for, according to the

University of Illinois Extension, the pumpkin, along with gourds, squash, cucumbers and melons, are all members of the cucurbitaceae family and considered to be fruits. What exactly distinguishes a fruit from a vegetable, I don't know. It has something to do with seeds and ripened ovaries, which is beginning to sound like something I really don't want to tackle.

Anyway, although in the fall there is ample opportunity to buy your jack-o-lantern or pie pumpkin from area farmers' markets, growing your own is especially fun for kids, who anticipate all the fun of Halloween along with watching the fruit develop. Most varieties need approximately 90 days to mature, so you'll have to plant early; obtain plants that have been started at a greenhouse or start them yourself at home.

First, whether you are growing or buying, you have to decide the color, size, and use before you choose one of the numerous pumpkin varieties. I will give you a short rundown on those I have grown.

Autumn Gold is an award-winning hybrid which matures and displays color early and weighs from 7-10 pounds. It is hearty in the north and can be used successfully for both eating and decorating. It makes a nice jack-o-lantern size.

Baby Boo (white) and Jack-Be-Little (orange) are miniatures which are edible but used mostly for fall decorative arrangements. They're fun for kids because they're hand-sized and high producers. If you plant them around a teepee-like arrangement of sticks, the vines will climb and cover, making a child's playhouse.

Rouge Vif D'estampes (Cinderella) is my absolute favorite. It's a brilliant red-orange color with a slightly flattened shape – it really is reminiscent of artists' renditions of Cinderella's coach – and weighs 25-30 pounds. It's great when stuffed with your favorite meatloaf or bread stuffing recipe and baked and is equally spectacular as a porch or mantel decoration.

Atlantic Giant and Big Max both grow to weigh from 50 to more than 100 pounds. You may have to cover them if there is danger of frost since they need 120 days before harvest. The Big Max has better color and shape, as Atlantic Giant tends to be slightly asymmetrical and of a faint orange tinge.

For the best in growing tips, I'd like to tell you the story of a 300-pound Big Max grown by my friends and super gardeners Milly and Jim O'Leary of Cornucopia. They planted their pumpkin patch after forming mounds of tilled soil which had been liberally enhanced with horse manure. As seedlings emerged, they pulled out all but two or three plants per mound and watered diligently. (Bury a topless tin can with holes punched in the bottom in each mound, next to the plant, and fill with water as needed. This waters the roots without wetting the vines.) As the weeks passed, they selected one particularly vigorous plant and removed all but one embryonic fruit from its vine, allowing the nutrients to flow to the survivor.

As fall approached, the patch as a whole was wondrous to behold with pumpkins of all shapes and sizes growing in abundance; but Big Max (BM) was definitely the star. He was allowed to remain on the vine until the week before Halloween, since he was destined to be a holiday gift for the O'Leary grandson in Winona, Minnesota.

Harvesting BM was a struggle of great proportions. The O'Learys, along with several able-bodied volunteers from a nearby tavern, rolled and pushed the tremendous Cucurbitaceae into an empty appliance crate. The crate was then skidded up two planks into the bed of the O'Leary's old farm truck.

After weighing in at Ehler's General Store, which involved much multiplying and subtracting of crate, truck, etc., BM's 400-mile journey began. Padding and props did little to discourage his rolling and bumping; and the O'Learys soon tired of people gesturing and shouting at them as they jolted along at the old truck's top speed of 35 mph.

It was all worthwhile however, when they had unloaded BM on their daughter's front porch and stood enjoying a cold beer while they waited in anticipation of the first reaction when grandson, Lars, came home from school.

At last he rounded the corner. He stopped dead in his tracks. His jaw fell open and his eyes bulged, as his backpack fell to the sidewalk. After much kissing and hugging, the grandparents watched proudly as Lars walked around the giant pumpkin measuring its girth with his small arms and pressing his tiny fingers into the deep ridges. Was there ever such a pumpkin? Were there ever such grandparents?

Then, as they all beamed down at him, he spoke for

the first time. Looking up with a serious expression, he said meekly, "What I really wanted was a jack-o-lantern I could carry."

To summarize –

1. When buying the seed or a pumpkin, select a variety which suits your needs. Remember the O'Learys.

2. Plant in mounds which have been fertilized.

3. Pull all but two to three seedlings per mound.

4. Keep surrounding soil moist.

5. Prune the vines to one pumpkin if you want bigger fruit.

I'm so relieved since I have found that pumpkins only grow in ground!

A spring night's dream

And sleep, that sometimes shuts up sorrow's eye
Steal me awhile from mine own company.

Shakespeare from "A Midsummer Night's Dream"

We were in the kitchen wrapping leftovers in sheets of plastic. I concentrated on deciding whether the containers were slated for the freezer or the refrigerator. I kept the planning foremost in my mind, saving all other thoughts to draw out when everyone was gone and I was truly alone. Time enough then to feel the empty house and hear the clock ticking for the first time. Time to remember the 43 years of our life together. Time to cry.

"Look at all this food," I said. Aside from what we had prepared, there were all the dishes that friends and neighbors had left.

"Sorry for your loss," they'd mumbled awkwardly as they handed me a casserole and a card that would surely contain a nominal sum of money. A strange thing, the ritual of death. I know in other cultures mourners are allowed to keen, wail, and even throw themselves on the casket; but neither my Midwest, Scandinavian genes, nor those of my neighbors, would permit such a display.

I suddenly remembered the mentally-challenged, grown son of a friend who, when his father died, stood by the casket, tears rolling unashamedly down his man/boy cheeks as he kept repeating, "God damn! Too bad about Joe!" While everyone shushed him and tried to get him to move, it occurred to me that he was the only one in the room who made any sense.

My reverie was shattered suddenly as one of my daughters asked, "Was Dad ever romantic, Mom?" Her voice seemed too loud in that quiet aggregation, and I struggled to shift my thoughts to this astounding new topic. I decided to be humorous.

"I guess he was; we had four children." I laughed, and all in the room nervously produced a slight chuckle and busied themselves with foil and plastic–pressing, pinching, folding.

"But that was just sex. Was he ever romantic?" she persisted.

Alone that night I sat in my chair. It had been a long, difficult day, but I had managed to pull it off in the manner that was expected of me: no dramatics, put everyone at ease, make sure everyone's presence was properly acknowledged and that they were thanked, hugged, and promised a call "if I thought of anything I needed."

I looked at the empty recliner a few feet from mine, half expecting to see him there, ready to exchange comments on how the day had gone. Then my daughter's question popped into my head and I leaned back, pleased at having to concentrate on something besides his absence. I closed my eyes and began to recall.

It was May of my freshman year in college. Aside from the difficulties of dealing with homesickness, adjusting to classes, and getting along with roommates and new friends, it had been a harsh winter. Fierce storms had arrived early and continued through to spring, making living difficult even for us dorm girls, who only had to make our way across campus. Then miraculously, the thawing rains came early and the snow banks morphed into rivers rushing through every ravine and ditch, in what seemed a frantic effort to reach Lake Superior. The sun shone brightly and the land bloomed with early flowers we'd all forgotten about: violets, mayflowers, arbutus.

The Memorial Hall girls moved their notebooks and texts outside to study for final exams. It was 1951, and we didn't know that too much sun could cause cancer and definitely wrinkles. Even we fair-skinned sisters stretched out our bodies like drying pelts during the hours of strongest sunlight. I winced as I remembered some of the resulting, painful burns, although we felt even the rosy glow of damaged skin preferable to our fish-belly look.

We discovered a low building behind the dorm that had a flat, metal roof. It was perfect! Not only would the metal reflect more sunlight, but the rooftop provided the necessary privacy for exposing more delicate parts of the anatomy and for conducting personal discussions beyond the earshot of unwelcome listeners.

"Sweet dreams of you," sang Patsy Cline from Mary's portable radio, as a large group of us lay arranged like hot dogs on a grill.

"Are you going out with him again?"

"If he asks me." Along with the miracle of spring had come a possible love interest after a winter that was, for me, as harsh in the area of romance as it was in weather.

"Do you like him?"

"Well sure, I just know him from French class. He's funny and really nice. He's a music major. In fact, he's singing at the Spring Recital tonight."

"You're going, aren't you?"

"Do you think I should? Won't it seem too forward? I don't even know if I like him that much."

"You're such a drip! (Nowadays the words nerd or dork would apply). You have to encourage men, you know." Everyone agreed with a nod as we all made one turn to the right to accommodate the moving sun.

"But I don't want him to think I'm chasing him."

"What if we all go together? We'll just be on a girls' night out on campus!" Everyone agreed with a nod, as we turned again, this time to accommodate someone stretching out a leg cramp. That settled, we fell silent to concentrate on the mystique of the rays.

Later when we descended from the roof, we noticed the lilacs for the first time. Nondescript bushes behind the building had recently become laden with blooms: heavy and cone-shaped like full bunches of grapes. Before going inside, slightly dazed and disoriented from the light and heat, we gathered bouquets of the fragrant, lavender flowers, bringing the spring inside to adorn our stuffy rooms.

I spent the rest of the afternoon like a sleepwalker. It was spring and life flowed through me like a warming liquid on a cold day, first heating the core of my body then seeping slowly into the extremities until it felt as if I could curl my fingers and hold my future as I'd cradle a cup to keep it from spilling.

That night, after we'd curled and perfumed in preparation for the recital, we snipped sprigs of lilacs to pin in our hair or wear in our buttonholes. Some even made small nosegays with ribbon streamers to carry. I thought it a little like something out of *Midsummer Night's Dream* as our giddy group trooped across campus to Wheeler Hall.

At the door of the recital room a professor's wife stood with her three little girls, dressed in their best and excited about going to an adult event. We stopped as one and twined lilacs in their hair or pressed a sprig in their hands to carry. As we entered the room I could see our mood spread like a mist over those already seated, as they smiled and pointed at our flower-bedecked group. Suddenly we were all friends in the possibilities of spring and the magic of the evening.

I remember little about the music I heard that night except the last piece. The boy I barely knew, but who would become my husband for 43 years, turned to look directly at me and sang, flawlessly, a rendition of an ancient Ben Jonson poem: "Drink to me only with thine eyes, And I will pledge with mine; Or leave a kiss but in the cup, and I'll not look for wine."

I was aware of faces turning to look and of gentle proddings from my friends, as if I hadn't noticed what was happening. His eyes kept mine and maybe it was the spring, an unexpected declaration to a lonely girl, the smell of lilacs, or even Shakespeare's mythical Puck dispensing his infamous potion, but I fell in love that night; and though sorely pressed at times, I never fell out of love with that boy.

I awakened with a start and realized that the emotional drain of the day had caused me to slip into sleep when I had just meant to close my eyes and remember. Was it just a dream of something that I wished had happened? But, now fully awake and with open eyes, I heard again his voice and smelled the lilacs and felt the warm spring breeze from the open window of the recital hall. I'd forgotten the whole incident over the years of mundane worries and triumphs of life but now that I have it again, it will become my fondest memory. I'm sure there were other romantic moments throughout the course of our time together; but in life, the first of anything is always the sweetest.

Help! I'm drowning in the dating pool!

With the divorce rate soaring, and women outliving men by a five-to-one ratio, it's no wonder that the print media abounds in articles similar to the one I recently saw entitled, *How to Jump Back into the Dating Pool.*

Of course I read it. Contrary to what most young people believe, after age 65 the libido doesn't automatically self-destruct nor, unfortunately, do older women become immune to that inherent, feminine tendency towards self improvement, mostly undertaken – let's be honest here, girls – in the interest of attracting the opposite sex.

Now, this was an article that would never appear on the pages of *Playboy* (not even if it were retitled, *Sure-Fire Pick-Up Lines* and accompanied by pictures of scantily clad, buxom wenches) because men don't obsess about their looks and are, generally, (warranted or not) pretty satisfied with their behavior.

I decided to do a little research on this so-called dating pool and, being of the non-technological generation, I went first to the dating section of the local Sunday paper. There were two pages of small print ads. The columns were categorized first by sex (no, not will or won't) with headings of Male, Female, and Optional. These categories were further broken down into age groups: 20s-30s, 30s-40s, and so on.

The women's requisites were, to my disappointment, very unimaginative, clichéd and too general to ever employ any workable method of elimination. They wanted men who were their age or older; walks in the woods; dinners at romantic restaurants; men who loved dancing; sensitive talks by the fire; and partners for travel. A friend of mine said that her only requisite was that prospective suitors have teeth. Later she even amended that to include false teeth. We women are a compromising lot.

The men got right to the point with their demands. Maybe it's because this male generation was used to hiring or being hired and, therefore, familiar with cutting out the dead wood from the start. Most all of the ads from men wanted women at least 10 years younger than they; asked for specifics like weight, height, and even hair color; listed bonuses such as good cook and likes animals (no cats) and partners for travel.

Basically the article promoted the same, old claptrap

that I had read in *Seventeen* when my age corresponded with the name of the magazine. "Be a good listener! Talk about him and the subjects that interest him! Smile often, and be good natured! Don't talk about former boyfriends, and – horror of all horrors – don't order the most expensive thing on the menu." For the more mature daters (those of us who've been around the block a few times), the advice varied from, "Don't talk about your kids or your operations!" to, "Don't discuss money – yours or his!"

Now I figured all of the above was pretty good advice, nothing new but, nevertheless, solid rules to observe in social situations with the opposite sex. And, being a rule follower, I mentally noted all the thou shalts and thou shalt nots of the dating commandments in the event that the occasion should ever again arise when I would need them.

Needless to say, unlike Ulysses' wife in Homer's timeless classic, I was not pursued by a constant queue of suitors. I was, however, convinced by well-meaning friends to participate in a couple of blind dates with men they said, "would be perfect for me." I never realized how low an opinion they had of me. I'll detail just one date to give you the idea.

Bachelor Number One met me at a prearranged restaurant for lunch. Just as I was opening my car door to meet him, he suddenly dove head first into his back seat and surfaced with a tie that had evidently been on the floor. It was rampant with many colored flowers and of the wide variety. It was rumpled, to be sure, but after a cursory inspection he decided it was okay and knotted it around his neck before he turned to meet me, obviously confident that the small addition had made him presentable, indeed dashing.

No need to worry about my hogging the conversation. Within the first five minutes I learned he was divorced, was a crop farmer, had dated a lot of women (many who had tried to borrow money from him even before they had slept with him. Imagine such effrontery! Maybe he was used to the money exchange being after the sleeping), and that he was losing weight because he was working so hard on his farm without any help.

He ordered first and pointedly selected the senior citizen special of the day. I thought fleetingly of perversely burdening him with the bill for a porterhouse steak or shrimp, but fell into line with the chicken gravy over rice. As we ate I realized he hadn't donned that tie to impress me but rather as a bib to save his shirt. I became fascinated with trying to identify previous dinners, some of which looked tastier than what we were eating.

He talked a lot about how hard it was to work all day in the fields and have to come home and cook his own supper and wash his own clothes.

"What about you?" Finally I was going to have my say. I would astound him with my knowledge of English grammar and the tricky nuances of pronoun agreement. I would engage him with clever repartee and throw in a few slightly bawdy stories to let him know I wasn't a prude. But as I opened my mouth to respond I was bombarded with questions.

"Have you ever lived on a farm? Can you drive a tractor? Are you a good cook? Do you have your own teeth? Evidently he had one of the same requirements as my friend.

I decided to take control of the conversation and announced, before he could take me down, pry my mouth open, and count my teeth, "Yes, I have my own teeth and I think you need to hire a housekeeper more than you need a girlfriend." I rose and slipped my sweater from the chair back.

"I guess I'll have to if you won't come," he mumbled. I think my interview hadn't gone well.

Subsequent dates may have gone a little better but no noticeable sparks, and if there were occasional sparks, they died for lack of fuel before they ever ignited into any kind of acceptable flame.

There were no quiet walks in the woods or long talks before a glowing fire. I despair of ever finding anyone who will discuss the challenge of tenses in lie and lay. The pool has grown cold and uninviting. I've come to the conclusion that I'm going to have to devise some kind of water wings for that dating pool because although I can tread water and sometimes float, I had forgotten one important thing; I never did learn how to swim.

A summer romance

*This morning the green fists of the peonies
are getting ready to break my heart.*

Mary Oliver

 By the middle of August the garden always looks overgrown and untended. The Gloriosa daisies and pink cone flowers have leapt from their assigned spaces and re-seeded themselves everywhere, indiscriminately; and leggy, five-foot malva have chosen to grow in the midst of the one-foot, purple petunias, disturbing the whole plan: The rich, velvety petunias were meant to provide a low border and bloom abundantly all summer long while each perennial had its season.

Oh, I know what it takes: a judicious pruning and the ability to pull out the rogue seedlings when I recognize them in the spring. But in April and May, I am so hungry for any flash of green signaling the return of life that I can't bear to pluck out the tiny foxglove and lupine that have struggled to withstand the snow and ice. *They've earned their space,* I decide and move on with my weeding. Sometimes I defend my weakness by bringing a politically correct theme into the argument I wage with myself: *I'll have an integrated garden.*

Every year, around the middle of April, when the first peepers sound from the pond, I open my bedroom window and vow that it will remain open until October, barring windstorms. Then I can lie in bed and watch the stars or the lightning in the night sky. I can smell the lilacs in June or hear the wind in the pines, and sometimes, even detect the passage of a wild animal stirring the leaves in the woods close by. It's like living in a tree house. Every night I fall asleep to the squeaking of the garden fountain as the bucket fills with water, tips to empty, then rights itself, over and over and over again, in its mission to sustain the never-ending flow. *I should oil that,* I'd always muse sleepily, but by morning I would have forgotten about it. And so it goes.

Then one spring he came, and the sun shone brighter and the nights grew softer. He laughed at my reluctance to pull flower seedlings as we worked the garden together. "They make a much better show if you put each variety together instead of having one here, and one there," he said. I could see the logic but wondered vaguely if putting on a show was what I had in mind. "You don't want the bee balm to grow over the stargazer lilies!" But that was the fun of the garden – to suddenly discover a beautiful bloom hiding in the shade. But of course he was right, and I marveled at having such a knowledgeable companion.

I carried two cups of coffee to the garden one morning and found him kneeling by the fountain with an oilcan. "This damn thing squeaks so loud it wakes me up," he said, a little churlishly. He was right, I knew, because I'd sometimes wake to see him standing by the window, his form seemingly caught in the surrounding branches outside, as if held in a lacey, dark frame.

But when the fountain was oiled and silent, I was the one who had trouble sleeping and found myself lying awake, unaware that I was straining in vain to hear the sounds from the fountain that might drown out the unasked questions and groundless worries that crept, unbidden, into my mind.

Then came September and, like a migrating bird, he was gone. The leaves turned gold and one by one the perennials dried to bleached stalks that turned in the wind. I left my bedroom window open longer than usual that year even though the nights were colder, and I often had to pull the comforter more tightly to my body. I just couldn't let the summer go. Sleep eluded me, and I kept asking myself, *What went wrong?*" never able to come up with a conclusive answer.

One cold night, as I lay bundled and wide-eyed, I suddenly heard again the familiar squeak of the fountain bucket. At first I didn't recognize the sound and it took a few seconds before I identified it. Then I smiled and was strangely calm and comforted. *It must need more oil,*

I thought, *Oh well, it's probably time to drain it for winter anyway. I'll oil it next spring. Summer is over,* I was finally able to admit to myself.

There's always next year! It's that age-old belief in the future that gardeners (and lovers) are wont to hopefully intone. I could still feel a faint smile lingering on my lips as I closed my eyes and for one last time that summer was lulled into a dreamless sleep by the sound of the bucket filling, then tipping, then righting itself, over and over and over again in its mission to sustain the never-ending flow. And so it goes.

A pot of red tulips

On a blustery, cold day – March 26, 2001

Snowflakes sharp as shards of glass
Tap my window, and as they pass,
The plodding deer, with slackened
Gait and lowered heads,
Search for cedars, dense and low,
Where they can crouch and
Make their beds.

Bare branches cringe before the gale
And sway to shield their unborn buds,
Lest they should fail and yield to
Winter's chilling wail.
A barren summer will forecast
Their useful time on earth has passed.

I wonder at my strength of will.
Can I endure and bend until
The birds return. Or will I break
Like severed limbs when north winds shake?

Then, deep in thought, I turn my head.
And from a spot beside my chair,
A flash of colors, green and red
Renews my hope, my spirit mends.

A pot of tulips from my friends!

An apple for Christmas

Here's to thee, old apple-tree,
Whence thou may'st bud, and whence thou may'st blow!
And whence thou may'st bear apples enow!
Hats full!—caps full!
Bushel-bushel-sacks full,
And my pockets full too! Huzza!

18th century English fruitful apple tree ritual

"When I was a kid, we were lucky if we got an apple in the toe of our sock at Christmas." Every family has an Uncle Joe or Aunt Minnie who unfailingly makes this comment as the kids sit amidst their embarrassment of toys on Christmas morning.

Hot tip, Aunt Minnie; if you promised the kids an apple nowadays, they'd expect a computer or at least one of its electronic offspring.

Although I remember getting a bit more than an apple in my sock when I was a kid, I am now of an age where I find myself, like Joe and Minnie, longing for a simpler time when we settled for less, but when, strangely enough, Christmas was more fun.

And a lot of that Christmas fun centered around apples at my house. Maybe it's their color, which always mirrors the holly berries, cranberries, and large, red bows on packages. Maybe it's because, here in the Northland, it's the one fresh fruit that, if properly stored, lasts into the winter months. Or maybe it's their versatility; you can decorate with them; make useful items of them; and eat them.

Have you ever cut thin slices of apple to dry and string for a Christmas tree garland or to twine into a wreath? Have you ever cut small holes in the stem ends of apples for candle holders? Have you ever participated in a competition to see if you could pare an apple with only one long peeling? My Mother used to throw those peelings, after the talented knife wielder had been praised, on the back lids of the wood-burning stove; and the house would be steeped in the tantalizing smell of cooking apples for days. (Now it's known as potpourri, and you buy it in a cellophane bag for $10.) Sometimes we made Christmas presents for our mother (and Aunt Minnie) by pressing cloves tightly together into the surface of an apple and attaching a ribbon from the top for hanging. This pomander (pom derived from French for apple) would scent their closets for months.

Of course, the meat of the fruit wasn't wasted. After the competition, apple pies, strudel, cakes, and cookies were baked for the holiday meals. From the pie crust scraps, we kids were allowed to make "the smallest apple pies in the world" baked in bottle caps. And who can forget the Christmas morning pancakes with a spicy, tangy covering of homemade apple butter?

I don't remember any apple carols, but I do remember singing with gusto, "Here we go a-wassailing," not having the slightest idea what wassailing was. Later I learned that this carol is of pagan origin and was part of a primal apple tree ritual where a concoction of hard cider, sugar or honey, and ale plus bits of roasted apple, were all mulled over an open hearth and poured on the roots of the tree (not before a goodly portion made it down the gullets of the participants). As an offshoot of this ceremony, baked apples are often floated in a punchbowl of eggnog or hot hard cider at Christmas parties. (Great care must be taken to prevent revelers from imbibing in too much liquid, lest they confuse the holidays and try to bob for apples, which makes a terrible mess.)

So let the apple take its rightful place among the fir trees and holly as a traditional Christmas symbol. Maybe you'll even exclude one computer game or video to make room for that apple in the toe of your young one's stocking. Aunt Minnie and Uncle Joe would be so happy! Merry Christmas and Huzzah!

Home for Christmas

Old men talk, young men die!

Ancient proverb on war

 He dropped heavily into the Greyhound bus seat, jackknifing his knees crazily until he could settle his feet under the seat in front and stretch his long legs, wincing, then relaxing with an imperceptible sigh. Negotiating the buses, taxis, even the streams of people on the city sidewalks had been draining, and he looked forward to the long bus ride, staring out the window as farm country rolled by, disturbed occasionally by sleepy, little towns, then eventually by his sleepy, little hometown.

He smiled at the lady next to him; but, sensing that long conversations and explanations might follow, he leaned his head back, closed his eyes, and, feigning exhaustion, let his mind struggle to erase luggage tags, time schedules and the pain in his left hip.

Home for Christmas! The past four Christmases had been spent with changing groups of buddies under various conditions, mostly intolerable. He'd learned to think of the holiday as just another day and had made a good job of it, sometimes not even noticing that it had come and gone until a package or card, hopelessly lost in the maze of military mail, would make its late and dismantled appearance: paper torn, re-taped in places, the contents stale or broken.

He hadn't been home since he'd left for the army, a cocky, immortal 18-year-old who'd never been far from the farm and longed for adventure. It was on a Greyhound, maybe this very one. His little sister had cried and clung to his hand. Ma had tears in her eyes too, but she talked brusquely and kept repeating, as much for her own comfort as his, "You'll be home on leave for Christmas." She didn't specify which Christmas, he thought wryly, because he'd barely had time to complete his basic training when the attack came, canceling all leaves and ready troops were shipped overseas. He thought he'd get home sooner, but he had spent time in foreign prisons, then was sent back to the States and moved from one grim hospital to another, not fit to be released. Now, at last, he was home for Christmas, but somehow feeling apprehensive.

Everything had changed. He knew that from Ma's letters. His brothers and sisters had left home to make lives of their own. Ma said she and his kid sister were just rattling around in that big house, so they had moved into town to a small apartment over a plumbing shop. He smiled to himself inadvertently.

THE CLOUD FACTORY

He thought about that house by the lake where they'd all lived together: the big porch that circled almost the entire building, the tumbling barn stubbornly protesting that "the old place" was still a farm. He could see the fall cornfield, all in stubble, but still exhibiting summer's rows that marched in line down to the cranberry bog. He could almost smell that sharp autumn air and his breathe caught in his throat as he imagined stirring up a flock of migrating ducks that had paused to feed on the withered berries. Soon the first snowfall would ensure good tracking for deer hunting season. Then his smile faded as the thought of his hunting rifle passed across the panorama of his daydream. "I don't think I'll ever be able to pick up a gun again," he mused. "Probably couldn't maneuver rough country with this fake leg, anyway."

He shifted in his seat to disperse the dream. So, what was home? Was it the house where you grew up? Was it family or your friends, for him both now scattered? Maybe it was the town, but it probably had changed too, except for the lakes and river. *They'd stay the same*, he desperately hoped.

He felt as if he were in a time warp where he had been left behind while everything else had moved on. Wouldn't it have been better to stay in the hospital and have a Christmas dinner in the cafeteria with the other maimed and broken misfits than to have this bitter reminder of how much he had lost and how life would never be the same for him?

His reverie was jolted by the bus's sharp turn and abrupt stop at the depot. The scene was the same, yet different.

There was Ma, grayer and more lined from worrying about her children in harm's way. "The kid," now a teenager, was taller, more womanly, and sported a pony tail and a faint line of lipstick. He could see their concern as it took him so long to descend the steps with his cane. Then his sister was on him, hugging and patting and chattering about Christmas and how they were getting a huge tree and didn't he think she was grown up? As for Ma, her eyes filled with tears and she said, brusquely, "I'm glad they finally gave you leave for Christmas."

He hadn't cried in battle, prison, or even in the hospital when his phantom leg ached and nightmares made him afraid to sleep. Now, strangely, his own eyes filled with tears, and he stooped to gather them both as he whispered in Ma's ear, "I guess I'm home... finally home for Christmas.'

That was the story of one of my brothers whose trip home for Christmas was delayed for two years after Pearl Harbor was attacked in 1941. Isn't it strange how little we've learned in the last 60 years as now, after 9/11, that story repeats itself across our country? As they say, only the places and dates have changed.

When calves danced

Some of my fondest childhood memories center around visits from my Swedish immigrant uncles who occasionally brought fresh dairy and produce to our family from "up on the farm." Milk and eggs were a given but sometimes the tightly-lidded syrup pail held a special milk that my mother mixed with the fresh eggs, a little sugar, pinch of salt, a generous portion of vanilla, and sprinkling of nutmeg for our favorite dessert. At suppertime, it would come out of the oven with a golden-brown, sugar-crisp topping. My mouth waters just thinking about it and my mind is alive with memories of the kitchen with its big black woodstove and the whole family around the table.

That special milk was a cow's first milk after calving or, as they said on the farm, "coming fresh." Although the calves needed that thick, rich, colostrum for a good start, a few cups were always put aside for a pan of what my Mother called "feastings" and what I preferred to call by the

Swedish name kalvedans, which means calves dance. Part of the enjoyment of the dish was picturing in my mind's eye those velvety infants on their hind legs, front hooves entwined, side by side, doing a sprightly circle jig around the mother cow. Sometimes my brother and I performed our own rendition, which definitely added a dimension to the experience.

When I tell this story, listeners sometimes get a pinched look and say something like, "I didn't know that was fit for human consumption." And I guess people used to eat many foods, mostly in their determination to use every part of whatever they had butchered or harvested, that are no longer fashionable or even palatable to some in this age of flash frozen, hydrogenated, franchised, pre-prepared, oxygenated, preservative-laden entrées (ergo, not fit for human consumption).

Oh, I'm not above throwing a frozen pot pie in the microwave or heating up a can of soup. I'm as busy as anyone; but I realize that what I'm gaining in time, I'm losing in flavor. What bothers me is I think a goodly portion of our population hasn't acquired a taste for real food or – horrors – may never have been exposed to it. Ask any kid below the age of 16 about macaroni and cheese and they'll tell you it comes from a box and is made with orange powder. Your good old boiled potato, mashed and seasoned with a ladle or two of the cooking liquid, has been replaced by dried, boxed flakes, laced with preservatives. And what of the brides who proudly place that beautiful Duncan Hines cake in front of their new husbands, secure in the knowledge (from TV) that, "He'll think you spent all afternoon on it?"

Then there's our penchant for stocking out of season foods in the supermarkets, just because we can. The only thing that January watermelon has in common with a field-ripened, July melon is they're both wet. The tastes of most hot house grown fruits and vegetables hardly resemble those harvested during their natural growing season; tomatoes are prime examples.

I don't know, maybe my taste buds – not as keen as they once were – are getting confused by a selective memory. I've baked many an egg custard since that kalvedans, but none has tasted the same. Am I missing the special milk? Or was the taste enhanced by the anticipation of a treat, when treats were scarce? Maybe it was the family camaraderie and the crazy dancing with my brother.

Maybe someday, when today's children are old, they too will reminisce about the flavor of Big Macs they ate while packed in those little, plastic stanchions at McDonalds. Maybe they'll wax nostalgic over the breakfast bar their mothers lovingly threw to them as they ran out the door to catch their ride to school. Maybe by then most of their meals will be taken as pills or injections. Maybe I'm glad I won't be there!

But enough of the maybes! Try some real mashed pota-toes, or bake macaroni and cheese with cubes of cheddar. Buy and steam some of our local, seasonal veggies, or make a dessert out of our plentiful apple crop (no fair picking up the Mickey D's pie in a bag). Experience and savor the flavors unhurriedly while in the company of people you love. You might not see calves dancing, but I'm sure you'll come up with your own enjoyable images to remind you of special foods and special times.

Ode to the lowly cow

O lowly cou (middle English), of genus bos
who neither types nor faxes,
You worry not of gain or loss or how to pay your taxes.
You care not how to ease your stress or when to take a pill.
You follow not the latest news of Hilary and Bill.
But standing still within your stall or hoof deep in the mud,
Through summer, winter, spring and fall,
content to chew your cud.
A bale of hay or pasture green, cow comforts of that ilk,
For meager care you are the queen of yogurt,
cheese, and milk.
Your virtues we extol aloud, and laud your capability
And if your output wanes, you're proud to show
your versatility.
For when toward the setting sun that placid
bovine marches,
She'll resurrect inside our bun
beneath the golden arches.

Jack

Jack hit the floor with both feet and lurched, half asleep, to the bottom of his bed. Straining to see in the half light of early morning, his fingers explored the quilt until he felt the reassuring shape of his gun housed in the leather holster. He quickly buckled it around his waist. It didn't matter that he wore it over his pajamas; he'd remedy that later. Right now it was more important to have the protection. He felt for his knife and carefully inserted it under the holster belt.

The hallway was dark, and he could barely see as he walked slowly in his bare feet, glancing from side to side for possible danger. His hand rested lightly on the gun handle and he moved with stealth and deliberation. Was he too late? Maybe he had slept too long!

No! There they were! The twin humps under the blankets didn't move, but he could hear their even breathing. They were still sleeping, unaware of the menace that loomed over them in the weak, first light of dawn. Now was the time to strike, and he didn't hesitate! "Mom, Dad, somebody has to get up and take care of me!" And so, another day in the short but intense life of Jack had begun.

While his parents were fumbling with cereal boxes, he completed his array of props which would hopefully bring him through the day unscathed. His policeman's badge was too heavy for the thin pajama material and hung like a pendulum, swinging as he moved. A set of nunchaku was tucked under his belt opposite the knife. His Twins baseball cap was firmly in place, and his medieval sword lay on the kitchen counter close at hand as he worked over his cereal bowl.

"He watches too much television," I once said to my daughter. But then I remembered my childhood when, without television, my brothers and I felt compelled to gallop around the barnyard on imaginary steeds, periodically turning in our saddles to shoot our smoking finger guns at the bad guys. Or the stance my brother took when he would suddenly quit weeding the garden to make a machine gun of his hoe and mow me down.

One day in the fall Jack proudly told me that he and his dad were going to go deer hunting. He used a very grown-up voice, which signaled that I was not to mention that he was too little to hunt. And I did respect his dignity but couldn't resist presenting him with a small challenge. I knew he loved to watch his Bambi video and so, as much to tweak his dad as to tease him, I said, "Oh, no! Are you going to shoot Bambi?" I was immediately filled with grandmotherly regret at my cruelty as I saw the look of consternation come over his face. He was clearly grappling with his first moral dilemma. But just as I was about to let him off the hook, the lines in his face relaxed, and I knew he had come to a satisfactory solution.

"Well Grandma," he said condescendingly, "You know I won't shoot any deer that talks." I accepted his explanation without argument. When he is older, we will have the same discussion. Only then I won't let him convince me as easily.

Maybe our violent media diet is affecting Jack. But I've seen him as happy to make muffins with his mother as to engage in slicing Kung Fu moves. Maybe our children are desensitized by our national obsession with guns. But I have observed that he is often more tenderhearted than his sister who plays with dolls.

In the meantime, his choice of lifetime careers changes from day to day or hour to hour. Sometimes he'll don one of his dad's work gloves and hang by one arm from the stair railing, mimicking the stance of the Waste Management engineer leaning from the back of the garbage truck to snag a can.

I've stood at construction sites with him as he has remained mesmerized with the process of pouring cement. Fortunately, his attention span didn't allow for us to watch it harden. Whatever his choice, I know he will succeed, because he is a deep thinker with a well-developed imagination.

Come to think of it, that one glove thing might not be such a bad idea. Look what it did for Michael Jackson!

So, in spite of what this grandmother may conclude about the state of today's children, Jack will greet each day as a ninja-cop-cowboy-knight-baseball player. And besides, both the cat and dog like him best!

$\mathscr{Life}$ and times at the $\mathscr{IGA}$

She shopped at the IGA. Sometimes I'd see her making her way down Bayfield Street, each step carefully rehearsed before executed, and she seemed to always end up at the grocery store, often just as I'd pull my car into the parking lot. After all, where else would she go? Why would an old lady who walked need gas? What could she possibly need from the hardware store? Did she ever stop at the Time Out Restaurant for a cup of coffee, or at Coco Bakery for a loaf of bread? That about exhausts the retail trade available in our small town; so I had to assume the grocery store was her primary destination.

I didn't know her and had no reason to single her out for observation. It's just that we often shopped at the same time – I on Sunday after a leisurely breakfast and in need of a weekend paper, she, obviously after church and in need of Sunday dinner. We went our separate ways in the store, wandering from bananas to tomatoes and back to the deli counter. At first, if our paths crossed I'd smile, but the simple amenity seemed to startle her, as if she should know me but couldn't remember. I soon decided it was better for all concerned to ignore her. It was a rationalization, but it seemed mutually agreeable.

I continued to notice her because she was one of those people who had gotten stuck in an era and continued to live and dress as if it had been too painful to move on. We all have high school buddies who still wear their letter jackets or relive a special prom, or wear their hair in a beehive. Maybe they want to hold on to a time when they were happiest. (On the other hand, I have a friend, Margaret, who is in her 90s and wears jeans and flip flops. Margaret has kept up and thinks that maybe her happiest times are yet to come, but that's just Margaret.)

My IGA friend obviously came from the fifties when women dressed to go out in public. She was in a beige suit with a yellow print blouse. The edges of her jacket lapels and cuffs seemed a bit grimy, but maybe it wasn't dirt but just wear from having been creased for so long.

She wore a pillbox hat with mangled flowers, too misshapen to identify a daisy or pansy; but the brim did allow for a few white curls to frame her face in a rather fetching way. I could see traces of pancake makeup in the downward creases of her cheeks, her lips were unnaturally red, and she had applied two precise circles of rouge.

She was small and thin. (They say stout women usually don't grow to be very old, so much for my longevity). Her legs were birdlike and her hose bunched at the ankles.

Beige patent leather pumps, cracked with age, completed her ensemble.

In spite of her dated look, she seemed in charge and overall spry. That's a word that has fallen out of use, but old people (and chickens) often used to be referred to as spry if they were in reasonably good health and still able to perambulate under their own steam. Come to think of it, there used to be a vegetable shortening called Spry, "use it for all your best cakes and pies." I wonder if they still sell Spry at the IGA?

At some point I looked down at my sweatpants and loose shirt and almost felt I should apologize for my inappropriate and frumpy appearance. For even though she dressed from a bygone era, she had maintained the dignity of her former station in life. Maybe she had been an influential Washburn clubwoman when that beige suit was fresh and stylish. Maybe she had held a job, or "went out to business" as my old aunt used to say about working women. Whatever her background, she didn't ask for help or sympathy and walked with her head high. Her attitude belied her shabby outfit. You had to admire that.

One day I turned down an aisle and saw her standing in front of the spice racks. She was holding a small container in her hands and adjusted her glasses for better scrutiny. I was prepared to steer around her, as usual, when she turned and held out the offending jar.

"Look at this," she said, "could this tiny jar of cinnamon possibly be $3.50?"

"Isn't that terrible? You'd think Marco Polo had just brought it back from the Spice Islands," I quipped, thinking myself very witty. She ignored the remark.

"I like a little cinnamon sugar on my morning toast, but not at that price." She caressed the red plastic cover for a few seconds and replaced it on the shelf. She grasped her cart handle and I moved on.

I thought about how I sometimes throw items into my shopping cart without even checking the price. Lord knows I don't have a lot of money, but surely I could buy that woman a jar of cinnamon. It's my favorite spice too. Oh, but how could I do that? She considered me a stranger, and something told me she'd be touchy about charity. Could I buy it and slip it into her bag? No, she might return it to the store when she unpacked the bag.

Still contemplating the difficulty in doing a good deed, I happened to pull in behind her at the check out counter, and I idly watched her deposit her few items on the conveyer belt. As she reached to retrieve her bananas from the bottom of the cart, I saw the red, plastic cover of the cinnamon jar momentarily breach the opening of her jacket pocket. She stood up and adjusted her clothes, brushing the pocket area slightly to ensure the presence of the purloined delicacy.

Scenarios raced around inside my head. I had just seen *Les Miserables* and saw my spry friend thrown into the Washburn County Jail even as Jean Valjean went to prison for stealing a loaf of bread. Would the shame of her deed haunt her for whatever life she had left like an open wound that never healed? Would she be banished from the IGA, eventually starving for lack of groceries?

Should I report her to the manager like a Nazi youth turning in her own parent to the storm troopers? Should I fail to report a crime and risk the fate of my own mortal soul?

Go! Go! I screamed soundlessly inside my head. *Make your escape and I'll keep your secret even if faced with water boarding.* (Did I mention I tend to get a little too dramatic?) Through all my inner turmoil my friend (for now she is my friend, for why would you do something as noble as this for a stranger or enemy?) is casually talking to the clerk.

"Is this the day for senior discount?"

Discount? Are you crazy? Run!

"No, Ma'am, senior discount is on Wednesdays"

"Isn't this Wednesday?"

"No, Ma'am, this is Sunday."

Just go! So much for you're having been at church, anyway.!

Finally she picked up her bag and made her way slowly out the door. Suffering the pangs of moral turpitude, my face had become flushed and I was breathing heavily.

"Are you alright, Ma'am?"

"Just ring me up and don't make any mistakes. Be sure you charge me for everything I've got." The clerk looked at me funny. *Did he suspect me of wrongdoing? Did I look guilty?*

I calmed down eventually and actually found the whole incident quite amusing. Had she decided that charging that price was already robbery, so why not participate? Desperate times call for desperate measures was my new mantra. I saw her many times thereafter, but we only exchanged short greetings or even a slight nod of the head. I stood behind her at the checkout counter many times, As far as I could see, she hadn't continued her larcenous ways. The price of that cinnamon had sent her over the top just one time, and that small jar of spicy goodness would probably last her for life. For all I knew she may be a secret millionaire. Before her groceries were totaled she always asked the same question,

"Is this the day for senior discount?" Occasionally she hit it right, and then I felt that bells ought to ring and confetti fall from the ceiling.

One day I realized I hadn't seen her for some time. In the line I tried to question the high school boy clerk.

"Do you know that elderly, small woman who used to always ask if it was senior discount day?" He shook his head.

"Do you know her name? She always carried a string bag for her groceries." He shook his head. Is it true that the elderly are invisible? Maybe this isn't even the same high school kid clerk. They all look the same. I let it go, as you learn to do with age.

I never did find out who she was or what happened to her. I assume she has died. Or maybe, sadly, she is confined to her residence, no longer able to roam the IGA at will.

Now, months later, I am once again in the IGA looking at the vast array of cereals. I'm holding a box of Honey Bunches of Oats with real clusters of nuts and honey and reading the proud claim: now double bunches. I turn to a young woman pushing her cart behind me and ask,

"What could possibly be in here that would make it worth $5.50?"

"It's the nuts," she replied helpfully.

"It certainly is," I replied.

She smiled at me sweetly, if a little condescendingly, and touched me briefly on the shoulder. I sensed that there had just been a passing of the guard, of sorts, and as she pushed her cart away, I readjusted my sweatpants, smoothed my shirt down over my waist, and called after her,

"When you tell this story, please remember to mention that I'm spry! Thank you."

What do northerners know about barbecue?

Years ago (this could get lengthy), as a young wife endeavoring to enhance my husband's career by using all the skills I had acquired over 25 years of marriage (I could brown hamburger), I volunteered to work at the Regional High School Music Festival which, at that time, was held at Northland College and sponsored by the college music department. There were hundreds of participants from a wide area who had registered for this event which included lunch. Providing this lunch had become a special project of The Northland College Dames.

The Northland Dames was an imposing presence on the campus at that time.

Comprised of male professors' wives and some local club women, particularly those whose husbands were on the Northland Board, the Northland Dames engaged in money making. I don't believe the organization exists anymore, since most wives have meaningful jobs that pay them and the purpose – mostly to give some status to these shadow dwelling women – no longer seems relevant in this society.

But I digress! I attended the planning meeting, naively thinking I would make my mark handling publicity or registration. I would perform so superbly that I would become known as "Laurie" and not just "Bill's Wife." Imagine my chagrin when I was one of 20 women handed the barbecue recipe and told to, "Have it at the student center by 11:00 a.m."

On Festival day, I watched my savory batch of BBQ sink into anonymity as the sturdy outdoor education professor's wife (I can't remember her name), wielding what looked like a canoe paddle, J-stroked it into the vast, simmering cauldron of generic sandwich filling. I was still "Bill's Wife."

However, I did recognize the superiority of the Dames' recipe over any of my previous formulas, and have used it for countless graduations, birthday parties, cookouts, etc. over the years. Some nameless Dame, now long in her grave I'm sure, is honored posthumously for her experimentation and research every time this recipe is used. I lay a symbolic wreath at the unmarked grave of the unknown BBQ recipe developer.

As I pass this treasured formula on to you, I feel it important to impress you with a sense of heritage.

5 lbs. hamburger

3 chopped onions

3-6 sticks celery (chopped)

1 bottle catsup (14 oz.)

1 can tomato sauce

¼ cup Worcestershire sauce

¼ cup prepared mustard

1/3 cup vinegar

3 tbsp. sugar (or less if you desire)

salt and pepper

– Sincerely, Bill's Wife

O Canada

Yesterday an article in our local paper dealt with Canada and our ignorance of and indifference to its culture, politics, and history. A Canadian writer I know referred to his own country as, "good old, grey-faced Canada," and that phrase seems to embody the general impression south of the border: dull and irrelevant, but dependable. Ask any U.S. citizen about Canada and I'd be willing to bet at least one of three words would be mentioned: bacon, hockey, and the @#% Canadian geese. I have a few more impressions, because I had the good fortune to live there for six years, and the newspaper article set me to thinking.

It was way back in the turbulent '60s when a Canadian friend phoned my husband, who was teaching high school music at the time. They had become friends at the University of Minnesota graduate school in St. Paul and had just received their Masters degrees that summer.

"We're building a grand, new branch of the University of Saskatchewan here in Regina," he said, "It's all set for you laddie, if you want to come, there's a job waiting for you." Now if you've ever been a teacher, particularly in high schools, you know that practically the only way to advance is to move, and we'd moved a lot; but this was a chance to break into college teaching and it also promised an adventure.

And so we moved lock, stock, and small, snappy dog to the capital city of Saskatchewan Province in the middle of the prairie. Our friend had not exaggerated when he referred to the University at Regina as grand. A great tract of land at the edge of the city had been designated for the project and truckload after truckload of fill and topsoil had been hauled to make hills and small valleys. Other vehicles transported full-sized hardwood and evergreen trees, and landscapers arranged the pleasant flow of shrubs, walkways, and flower beds around the initial two, modern buildings. We arrived in time to witness the planting of the trees. It was an awesome sight as trucks carrying 30-40 foot trees rumbled down the road in front of our house, their branches waving in response to the potholes.

The Reginans weren't as impressed with the transformation as we were, however. After all, they had already built a park in the middle of the city that had not only a good-sized hill, but a small, man-made lake with an island in the middle. You didn't catch them sitting around complaining about their surroundings.

The people were among the friendliest I've met. There was a strong Scottish contingent in Saskatchewan, which accounted for our friend's use of the laddie familiarity, and since Canada had not yet restricted its immigration quotas, as had the U.S., our home street alone had global representation. Our neighbors on either side were the Wongs from China; the Gavins from Scotland; our dear English friend Millie Wilson and dog Brock; and Mr. Blackman, who was our daughters' violin teacher and who Anne Gavin in her clipped, accent had designated as, "from the Orkland Islands off Scotland, where they're hardly civilized."

We all got along, however, and enjoyed block parties and ended up helping each other through difficult times. The newly arrived Englishmen at the University could be stuffy; we all smarted a bit at their constantly referring to us as, "You colonials." But then, maybe it was just an example of that famous British humor. Some of our own countrymen had the habit of prefacing their comments with, "Well, in the States..." which didn't go over that well either.

In the spring of our first year there, we prepared for graduation with great excitement, because the Prime Minister, Lester Pearson, was going to be the speaker. I managed a seat at a good vantage point and watched in awe as the parade of distinguished professors and government officials, all dressed in the regalia of such exotic places of higher learning as the Universities of Edinborough, Cambridge, Yale, McGill, Oxford, and Minnesota (the last example being that of my husband in his plain, black robe) progressed slowly down the aisle. Some wore red, satin robes with matching hats, others purple satin trimmed with fur. All were led by some official in red knickers and a tri-cornered hat with a gold mace in his hand, which he maneuvered like a head drum major.

"Where's the Prime Minister?" I whispered to my Canadian companion.

"There!" She pointed to a short, oldish man in a plain black robe like my husband's.

"Where do you suppose the secret service men are?" I said as I looked over the crowd.

"What secret service?" came the reply.

"Those who guard him from an assassination attempt." There was a moment of comprehension before she looked at me in wonder.

"Why would anyone want to kill Lester?" she replied.

Of course, we Americans were living in a decade of tragic assassinations and, sadly, almost accustomed to them; but I've often wondered how people so alike and who share an unarmed border can think so differently about politics and politicians. It's more complicated, I know, and there isn't an easy answer.

A couple years later, Pierre Eliot Trudeau, the new, dashing, French Canadian Prime Minister was visiting Regina and would be making a speech in the park. *Things will be different,* I thought, *he's more controversial, more worldly.* I listened to his talk and decided I'd try to shake hands with him. I ran toward his entourage, going over the tops of picnic tables in order to skirt crowds of people, and burst into a clearing directly in front of him. No one threw me to the ground or drew a gun.

"Bonjour," he said and held out his hand.

It would require much more space to discuss how much I appreciated a government that took care of its people's health and insurance needs. Suffice it to say that I came to respect and love Canada for many reasons. So what am I doing back in the United States? No matter how wonderful Canada is, it's not America and I love my country more, warts and all.

Death on a June day

Dance There Upon the Shore
W. B. Yeats

It was a day on Lake Superior that answered that "Why do you live here?" question often asked of us locals in January or February. At last it was June. The lupines were in bloom: stately groups standing, unselectively, in quiet grandeur along every highway, path, and trail. Icy winds had been replaced with a warm breeze that was gentle enough to just ruffle the water lapping against the shore on Bayview Beach, but strong enough to keep away any bothersome insects.

My best friend and I were on our morning walk, which alternated between the forest road and the beach. My friend preferred the beach because he could take several cooling dips in the lake during the course of traversing from Bayview to Sioux River. My best friend is, of course, my golden retriever, Buddy. People tell me he has the typical disposition of his breed: affectionate, docile, eager to please, but with just a touch of stubbornness if pressed. I know that he smiles (with full disclosure of his upper teeth) and talks (in dog language, to be sure, which I can translate but not speak) and that he greets me every morning and every time I come home with enough joy and enthusiasm to make me think myself the most desirable person on the planet.

We like to go to the beach early, before bathers and picnickers arrive. With the place to ourselves, I can let Buddy run free. I love to watch him race away, full out, releasing some of that pent-up energy he can't expend in the yard. He resembles a shaggy, red racehorse then, legs extending in a graceful gallop, traveling at least three to four feet with each stride. He'd generally complete about five of these trips, running away, then back to me to see that I was still following at my own pokey pace. He only deviated from this route if he was attracted by an interesting smell or to make a deposit, considerately away from the beach, beyond the tree line.

We had just finished the loop and were at my car. Buddy sniffed around bushes lining the access road, while I opened the hatch for him and brushed the sand from my feet. Suddenly the bushes burst apart, and a fawn leapt onto the road and bound away down the beach. An astonished Buddy hesitated for only a second before he took off, sending up a spray of sand as he launched into the chase. I yelled, "NO!" at the top of my lungs, but to no avail.

I shouted his name, "Buddy, no!" I called sternly, answered only by the fawn's bleat and the dog's bark that got weaker as they sped down the beach.

Soon I could no longer see them and I ran to the swampy area in back of the tree line. There, standing stock-still, ears and nose twitching, was a doe, obviously the mother. She didn't start, and I turned back to the beach still calling for Buddy. But my 76 years have rendered me in poor shape for rescuing, and I sat in the sand trying to get my breath – at this point, I could hear neither bleat nor bark. I scanned the beach both ways, and strained to hear any signs of struggle. Through the sun's glare I detected movement on the lake's surface out a good 20 to 30 feet.

I made out the shape of the fawn's head, with Buddy's shaggy one just behind it. I waded out, still calling and demanding obedience. I hurried faster into the icy waters of Lake Superior when I got close enough to see that Buddy, himself, was looking a little panicked. Then, making a sudden decision to save his own skin and obey me, he turned abruptly and began laboriously swimming toward me. The fawn's head disappeared and I didn't see it again although I stood peering into the sun for a long time.

Finally we made our way to the car, my labored breathing the only sound on the beach now. "Get in," I ordered unkindly. I indicated the hatchback and Buddy jumped in with lowered head, sinking down in exhaustion, waterlogged and chastened by the tone of my voice. "I hate you Buddy!" I gasped, as I slammed the door, and climbed into the driver's seat. I sat, calming myself, and desperately trying to come up with different scenarios that had the fawn surviving: If Buddy hadn't injured it, it could have survived and made it to shore without my noticing it. I knew this was highly unlikely, and the truth hit like a blow when I stopped to turn onto the highway and saw the mother standing alone under the trees.

The beautiful June day was spoiled, and I did little to improve the tenor of the afternoon. I brooded in my chair. I tried to excuse Buddy by reasoning that he was acting like a dog. How many times had I watched and laughed as he chased the shore birds along the beach? They'd skim the water's surface, then perch on the sand, only to flit away when he was almost upon them. It was a sanctioned game. If he became confused, it was my fault.

Besides, fawns are killed all the time. In the spring they're easy prey for coyotes, bears, cars; but does that somehow make the horror of witnessing a defenseless, small thing being driven to death legitimate and not worth noticing? What about hunters who yearly drive and chase animals to their deaths? And how could I hate my dear Buddy when minutes before I had loved him? This must be the way mothers of serial killers feel about their children. Had I made a person out of my dog? I shook my head, realizing that I was sinking into the morose, over-analytical thinking that my daughters call, "Mother getting weird again."

At five o'clock I turned on the television to learn that my favorite news journalist, Tim Russert, had died suddenly;

a tornado had taken the life of a two-year-old in southern Wisconsin; and ten more U.S. soldiers had died in Iraq. The world would mourn Tim Russert, with good reason. A family and a town would mourn the child. Ten families and ten towns and ten states would mourn the soldiers. I alone would mourn the fawn, so briefly on this earth. The deaths on that June day couldn't and shouldn't be compared. But death is equally final for the claimed, no matter who or what they are.

Buddy came to the side of my chair and nudged his nose under my elbow for attention and affection. His kind, brown eyes seemed to say he was sorry, although he didn't know for what; or maybe I just wanted him to be sorry, so I could forgive him. He laid his head in my lap and enjoyed an ear rubbing. We'll go for our walk again tomorrow, but maybe not to "dance there upon the shore" for a long time.

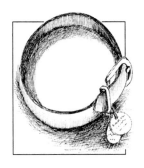

For Buddy

I've seen him smile, a toothy grin,
And taste the air on a windy day
As if to fuel his prancing frame
For the circling and chasing about to begin.
Conducting my walk was his favorite play.
Five miles to my one was his usual game.

A reprimand, however mild,
Would draw a sigh and lowered gaze.
But with a pat and friendly voice,
Forgiveness followed and, beguiled,
I'd watch him lift his paw and raise
His eyes with love to me, his choice.

For even Argos, Ulysses' friend,
Could never match his loyalty.
Now, still body and visage grim
I gather close. But tears won't mend
Or bring his joyousness to me.
This lifeless pelt is not how I'll remember him.

What's up with all the kissing?

*Before you kissed me only winds of heaven
Had kissed me, and the tenderness of rain –
Now you have come, how can I care for kisses
Like theirs again?*

The Kiss by Sara Teasdale

President Obama was about to make an all-important speech explaining his health care plan. I was seated in my recliner in front of the television well ahead of time, because I enjoy watching all the congressmen and women enter and take their seats. I always experience a feeling of pride and patriotism, much more so since the last election, when the Sergeant-at-Arms announces, "Ladies and gentlemen, the President of the United States."

I watched as Nancy Pelosi entered and was kissed by all her colleagues. (Did anyone ever kiss Tip O'Neal as he was about to chair a session?) I watched as Olympia Snow was bussed by fellow and sister senators. (Who kissed Paul Wellstone?) I noticed a positive rain of kisses on Michelle Obama; I even witnessed chaste pecks on the cheek for our Secretary of State, Hilary Clinton. (I don't remember seeing anyone kiss Henry Kissinger). It seemed all the women connected to that august body by either career or marriage were being kissed with varying degrees of enthusiasm.

Then the President entered and as he made his way to the podium, he too stopped to plant one on the cheek of every female in his path. Is it some vast, left-wing conspiracy designed to distract the gullible public while the liberals grab more power, or is it a subtle terrorist plot? Is it a manifestation, intentional or not, of the glass ceiling, meant to set the women apart as the weaker, less influential members of Congress?

When did this surge of osculation begin? In 1933 when FDR picked Francis Perkins as the first female cabinet member did he seal it with a kiss? In 1917 did Woodrow Wilson smooch Jeanette Rankin when she took her seat as the first woman in Congress?

Of course the public kissing of both sexes has long been a custom in other countries. The French military ritual of bestowing a kiss on each cheek is an integral part of the ceremonial presentation to honor bravery.

President Jimmy Carter was ridiculed in the press for

returning a kiss from Russian Leonid Brezhnev, the General Secretary of the Communist Party between 1964 and 1982. Brezhnev was noted for giving male colleagues the full liplock kiss. The press joked that Brezhnev commented of Carter, "Rubbish politician, but what a kisser!"

The Italians have made famous the Biblical Judas kiss, or should I say that the media has in *The Godfather* and *The Sopranos*. Come to think of it, I'd place the blame for this whole state of affairs on the media.

Ever since Ronald Reagan portrayed the role of President in the '80s, the Hollywood influence has been seeping into our hallowed halls of government.

Of course, we've all become addicted to television talk shows and accustomed to the host kissing all the female guests while the males have to be content with a handshake or an awkward, aborted hug. So has Hollywood finally come to the U.S. Congress, or has Congress become one huge talk show with an endless parade of celebrity and wannabe celebrity guests?

It's time to take a stand. Let's postpone the wrangling over taxes and budget and clear up a shady area for our Senators and Congressmen. Some brave soul should introduce a bill that all greetings, whether to males or females, within the Capitol should be concluded with a kiss.

I'm sure it would result in great discussion. Maybe someone would then propose an opposing bill saying that all greetings should conclude with a handshake. The deciding vote would result in a clear cut policy.

Could anyone be accused of torture if forced to kiss Dick Cheney? Would refusal to kiss Barney Frank carry the politically incorrect label? Would a kiss to Queen Elizabeth result in censure for touching royalty?

What really does a kiss imply that a handshake doesn't cover? Glad to see you? You're my friend? You're my enemy but I'm trying to hide it? A kiss implies all of those but also might include certain sexual signals open for interpretation. And we all know, it's that interpretation that gets many of our politicians in trouble.

On fighting progress... and losing!

It wasn't breaking news like the downfall of AIG or the GM closures. It was a mere mention I heard by chance on my car radio.

"Hershey's Candy Company has announced they will no longer make Zagnut Bars in the United States and will move their operation to Mexico."

What does this mean? Do we have to risk the drinking water and the drug lords, to say nothing of swine flu, for the privilege of buying a Zagnut? Who made this decision? Was it some fresh-faced marketing graduate who probably only eats trail mix who used demographics and market analysis to recommend this action? Did "they" develop a profile of the typical American Zagnut buyer only to find that it was an overweight, elderly, lady in the backwoods of a northern state who was nostalgic about her childhood treats?

I seem to remember my old Aunt Minnie reminiscing about the sticks of horehound candy she could no longer get.

Had I become Aunt Minnie? What on earth is horehound? I must calm down, as I understand that you probably don't know what I'm talking about.

Let me give you some background. Zagnut is an unassuming little candy bar of a peanut brittle consistency that offers an alternative to chocolate covered confections. It is coated with an orange, fibrous material that I always thought was a coconut derivative. Oh, it probably couldn't compete with Snickers or Milky Way, but it had its place in the candy bar line. It's been on the market since 1930 and since I was born in 1932, it has become just one more constant in my life that now alas, seems to be crumbling.

Truth be told, maybe it isn't so much the demise of a candy bar that is bothering me, but that for me, Zagnut has triggered another instance of the sign-of-the-times. It's this consuming need in all aspects of our modern lives to equate change with progress; you don't always need change to progress. Nowadays everything has to be faster, easier, and newer. We have to multitask, innovate, and escalate when maybe we should try repetition, concentration and experimentation. Now I'm beginning to sound like Johnny Cochran.

Of course PCs and the Internet are to blame for this feverish technological pace. They are directly responsible for the decline in book sales, libraries, and newspapers. Soon bookstores will be relegated to sleazy, back streets where mole-like proprietors will dust mildew-smelling volumes for collectors or for really old people who still haven't learned to use a computer. I used to be comforted by the fact that you couldn't curl up in bed with a good computer, but now you can. We have Blackberries, laptops, notebooks, and the latest – Lollipops (Why won't they leave our candy alone?), all of which can be taken anywhere, even into the bathroom!

Libraries have already changed with the times, and not only sport the electronic card catalog but banks of PCs for public use. How much longer before the only shelved books will be PC manuals? After all, you can research any subject online faster and more extensively.

And what about our newspapers? Editors are finding a huge decline in subscriptions; and in all fairness, which is more appealing: to wade in a snow bank to extract a wet newspaper or to sit inside at your computer with a cup of coffee while you access your local publication online? Also, past editions of the local paper can be easily restored on the screen – really helpful for a local history project or when you can't remember the time of an event and yesterday's paper is lining the cat box.

It's at this point in my tirade that, feeling like a traitor to my generation, I went to the Internet and typed in Zagnut. Immediately pages of information flashed to the screen. I learned that it was, "a solid, midrange performer of a candy bar, a good backup when maybe you don't want an Almond Joy or maybe want a little more crunch than a 3 Musketeers" (take that, fresh-faced young market analyst).

To my increased surprise, I found the Candy Blog and was gratified to read the pages of quotes from real people of all ages who, like me, missed and were looking for Zagnut. People like Greg from Orlando who said,

"My favorite candy bar of all time. Maybe because I was introduced to it at the town community pool by a girl in a bikini that I had a crush on when I was about 13 years old!"

Oh, Greg, I suspect something more than a sweet tooth sparked your need for sugar!

Barbara said, "I think the Zagnut is by far one of the all-time best candy bars ever made!!"

Julie frantically wrote,

"Where are the Zagnut candy bars!!!!!!"

In answer were pages of Zagnut sightings from candy fans who had found them in obscure gas stations and convenience stores from the Ozarks to Oregon.

So, what do I want, aside from a case of Zagnuts? I don't advocate throwing all our electronics into Lake Superior, although I have a couple VCRs, barely used but now obsolete, that I'd like to trash. I just wonder if we really need another new communication device. So far we can email, Facebook, Myspace, blog, cell phone, text message, Blackberry, Twitter, and pretend to excel at something on a Wii. I probably haven't named all these devices, and a new crop of prototypes is being developed as we speak. But so many of the above have been abused that new regulations are being placed on them everyday, particularly on their use while driving.

Why can't our best and brightest young scientists concentrate on improving the safety of our vehicles, alternate fuels, electronic devices for handicapped people, improving agriculture, bringing the infrastructure into the new millennium, etc. We don't need any more fad gadgets. But, of course, it's all about marketing and making money.

Poor, old Zagnut just couldn't compete with Snickers any more than I can compete with the march of progress (time). I don't know though, after reading the comments on the Candy Blog, we might be facing a time when bootleg Zagnuts could be a thriving business down on the border at Bush's wall.

In closing, shame on you Hershey's for moving your operation to Mexico, leaving about 300 Pennsylvania workers without jobs. As for those Mexican workers, I can only paraphrase the famous words attributed to Marie Antoinette and say,

"Let 'em eat Zagnuts." The lucky stiffs. Me? I'm just going to try to find some horehound candy in honor of old Aunt Minnie. Maybe if I go on the Internet...

Is pie throwing bullying?

I enjoy making pie. I've had years of experience and have discovered and employ all sorts of shortcuts and techniques, so I can turn one out in a timely fashion. I can't, however, subscribe to that old adage, "It's easy as pie." It is by no means a quick, easy, last minute dessert.

I believe, in fact, that because it is so time consuming, the pie is going the way of homemade dill pickles or home churned ice cream. Soon there will be no one left who knows how to bake one from scratch. Mrs. Smith's frozen pies will reign in that world, and mothers, at the end of a meal, will even resort to handing diners one of those flat little apple pies in a bag from McDonald's.

That's one of the reasons why every year I'm happy to participate in the region's Pie & Politics night at Lake Superior Big Top Chautauqua. Here at last is a tribute to the women and men who still bake pies. Oh, it draws its share of bakery and Mrs. Smith's, but for the most part the quality and variety is something to behold.

Again this year the array was mind-boggling, however, the audience for the politics part of the evening was treated to a pre-speaker DVD that I found a little disturbing. It was meant to be entertaining. It showed a group from our area, in Madison to represent Northern concerns, as they met our area State Representatives on the steps of the capitol and threw pies in their faces. It's the sort of thing that's sometimes done in schools to "honor" certain teachers, and it's akin to the dunk tank at our fairs and celebrations. When and where did this behavior start? Off to the Internet...

During the silent movie era in the 1910s and 1920s, the action in comedies had to be enhanced by sight gags and the oldest form of humor, the classic slapstick (considered to be low-brow or kid stuff), was born and used repeatedly in Mack Sennett comedies. Mabel Normand, America's first queen of comedy, was often given credit for inventing pie throwing and did indeed determine that a custard pie worked best for this activity.

I have a lemon pie recipe that calls for a dozen eggs, four lemons, and requires three sojourns in the oven before completion. I can assure you that in my presence, anyone thinking of throwing one of my lemon custard pies in someone's face would soon find a dent in their skull from my mother's trusty rolling pin (fashioned in one piece from sturdy oak).

What do we call this pie throwing activity? Is it good,

clean, fun for some? Is it hazing? Bullying? Is it just a practical joke? And on top of everything else, victims are expected to be good sports and enter into the spirit of the occasion. It's been my experience that being a good sport usually ends in someone being diminished in some way. Sounds like bullying to me.

Don't we have the much touted zero tolerance for bullying in our schools? I've heard that students nowadays are sometimes suspended from school for pushing, and now we even have laws about cyber bullying. I've further heard that respect for adults seems to be a big concern among parents and teachers. What does it say to our children when we single out our elected officials or our teachers for a form of ridicule? That's what it is because no matter the severity, bystanders laugh at you and your condition. Maybe pie throwing offshoots will take to waiting outside hospitals to pie the doctors, or outside courtrooms to pastry the lawyers. Let's not exclude anyone.

The group in the recent Madison incident stressed the fact that their pies were merely a mixture of some sort of biodegradable froth and paper and therefore not harmful to the environment. So the poor victims didn't even get slammed with something that tasted halfway decent. I can't think of a single kind of pie that isn't environmentally friendly. I suspect that the throwers didn't want to take the trouble and expense to use real pies.

How much more receptive would these representatives have been had this group presented them with a piece of pie made from Northern Wisconsin apples or berries and a glass of cold Wisconsin milk?

Let's have zero tolerance here, or if we insist on this low brow sport, there ought to be a law (maybe our own Bewley and Jauch can write one) stating that groups proposing this sort of activity must bake their own pies I suggest that three-step lemon pie of mine with the cooked meringue).

I've even got a title for the bill: *Remember the ala mode!* Do you think I'll be pied for that one?)

Lemon meringue pie

Pie Crust: Your favorite pie crust recipe for one 9-inch shell

Roll and arrange pie dough in 9-inch pie pan. Freeze the crust until hard, about 40 minutes. Heat oven to 350°. Line frozen crust with foil and fill with pie weights or dried beans. Bake on a cookie sheet for 40 minutes, remove foil and weights and bake until crust is golden brown and feels dry (another 20-30 minutes). Whisk an egg with 1 tsp. water. Brush on bottom and sides of crust and return to oven for about 3 minutes until egg is set and dry.

Ingredients:

6 large eggs

1½ cups sugar

½ cup fresh lime juice (from 4-6 limes)

¼ cup fresh lemon juice from two lemons
Grate zest before juicing.

1 cup heavy cream

1 tbs. grated lemon zest

Whisk together eggs and sugar, then whisk in lemon and lime juices. Whisk in cream and lemon zest. When the crust is done, pour the filling into the crust without removing it from the oven, reduce the oven temperature to 325°, and bake the pie until the center is just set, about 50 minutes. Cool on rack and refrigerate until cold, at least 6 hours. This part of the pie can be done a day ahead of time, with the meringue added the day it is served.

Meringue Ingredients:

1½ cup firmly packed brown sugar

½ cup water

¾ cup egg whites at room temperature (from 6 eggs)

¼ tsp. cream of tartar

Put brown sugar and water in saucepan and fit with candy thermometer. Put egg whites in mixing bowl with cream of tartar. Boil sugar until thermometer reaches 254°. Whip egg whites about 30 seconds then very slowly pour about 1/3 of the sugar mixture over the whites, beating constantly. Add remaining sugar mixture and beat until absorbed and the meringue is voluminous. Arrange on the pie and put on lowest rack of oven. Turn on broiler and brown, watching carefully and turning often until of desired color.

A moral dilemma

The class had just ended. Every day about five minutes before dismissal time, the same students adjusted their postures from the usual, half-reclining positions to an adaptation of the racers' starting form. They didn't utilize the conventional poised toe and bent knee, but innovated a form involving one buttock poised on the chair's edge with the right leg bent and ready to lever them toward the door for a fast getaway. This exercise had just been accomplished. Some class members were packing their book bags, while others had stopped to visit.

Barbara was packing her briefcase. There was the usual pile of exercises to be corrected and the faded textbooks displaying curled, paper markers that looked like panting tongues. As she snapped the lid, she was aware of someone standing at her elbow. One of the dismissal sprinters had been left behind.

"Can I talk to you, Mrs. Walker?"

"Sure! What can I do for you?"

"Well, give me a passing grade in this class for one thing." He sort of smirked as though he had made a clever comment.

"Didn't we talk at the nine week period? I think I indicated then that you were in trouble and needed to make some drastic changes. It's a little late now. We only have two weeks of school left."

"Yeah, I know, but my marketing teacher said I should come and talk to you."

"About what?"

"Well, you know, I'm doing okay in my marketing classes, but if I flunk your class, I won't graduate."

"Jim, I used practically the same words to you seven weeks ago, and you did nothing about it."

"Yeah, well I've been pretty busy, and you know I don't need this writing junk to do a marketing job anyway."

"I'm sorry! There's nothing I can do to change the record of the work you've done. You could have changed it, but I can't!"

He snatched his books from the table he leaned against and walked, stiff with anger, from the room. As Barbara turned the corner into the hall, she saw Jim standing with his girlfriend by the lockers. "She's flunking me, so I won't graduate!"

"What a bitch!"

They were silent as she walked past, but she could feel their eyes like lasers boring into her back. It was a relief to reach the solitude of the small cubicle which served as her office. It was three-thirty and she didn't have any more classes, but just as she opened her plan book to prepare for the next day, Dick Bremer, the counselor, poked his head around her cubicle wall.

Dick was a handsome man with startlingly white hair and weathered complexion. He was a sportsman and always had anecdotes for the male students and staff about his tree stands or deer camp or fishing trips to Canada. He was considered a good guy, even by the women.

"Did Jim come to see you?" he opened.

"Yes he did, but he left it too long. He can't change his grade now."

"Yeah, I know, darn kids anyway."

"He's hardly a kid, Dick, he's twenty-five years old."

"Well, he's had a lot of problems. I think everyone concerned would like to have a staffing on this, talk it all over and see if we can come up with something." His tone was unctuous.

"We have a policy. I can't think of a better instance where it applies. What's there to talk about in a staffing?"

"Well, you know, just make sure we've covered all the bases. I'll let you know when it is."

They gathered in the conference room. The division chairperson, Mary Klein, the major marketing instructor,

Stan Howard, Good Guy Dick, and Barbara sat around the table with mugs of coffee. There was a considerable amount of small talk with everyone hoping the friendly overture would soften the confrontational opera about to begin.

"Well, we have a problem with Jim Benson. It seems he's failing Communications. What are your thoughts on this, Stan?"

"Now Barbara, you know I'm not about to ask you to pass someone who has done failing work, but the kid is doing fine in marketing and that is what he came here to learn. I just think it's a shame that a general education class should keep him from reaching his goal."

"Why do you call him a kid? Because he acts like one? Because he displays the responsibility of one? And aren't the general education classes part of the Marketing Program's curriculum? And wasn't he aware of that when he registered for the program?"

Stan set his mug down and moved forward in his chair. His affable smile had faded, replaced by a deep frown bisecting his forehead. "Some of these students come to us knowing only failure. They hated academic subjects in school but liked numbers. So we work with them and they have a little success and even get to feeling good about themselves. Then we pull the rug out from under them because they can't do the very thing they hated in the first place. We're not a liberal arts college, for Pete's sake. We're training people for jobs." Beads of sweat had formed on his upper lip and his mouth seemed to have produced too much saliva.

"I'm aware that we're training people for jobs, but what happens on the job when Jim is asked to do something he doesn't like or even hates? Can he just ignore it, not do it? Is his employer going to allow that the kid has had a rough time and give him a raise to compensate? I gave him every opportunity to get help, to do alternate assignments, and he couldn't be bothered. In my opinion, we're not doing him any favors by giving him a gift." Barbara's voice sounded shaky, and she silently cursed her vocal chords for deserting her.

Stan swiveled in his chair as if dismissing the whole group as not worthy of his presence. Mary Klein looked nervous and leaned forward. "We've all agonized over this before, and we certainly can't ask Barbara to change a grade. On the other hand, we have to be the student's advocate. Barbara, is there any way we can give Jim some makeup work, even if it takes the summer to complete, and offer him the option of a delayed diploma?"

She was sapped. She hardly dared reply. For all his altruistic soundings, she knew Stan was more worried about the statistics showing the number of graduating students than he was about whether Jim had reached his career goals. Although no one recognized it, she was a better friend to Jim than either Stan or Dick. If she had voiced these opinions, she would have been labeled a troublemaker, and that would have been the mildest adjective used.

With a shrug of resignation, Barbara signaled her assent. Stan and Mary stood immediately before she changed her mind and mumbled some platitudes about compromise and how productive it was to be able to talk out a solution. Dick leaned over and patted her shoulder. "This'll work out better, kiddo. Now you won't have to have him in class next year taking it over again." He gave her an exaggerated wink.

She walked back to her cubicle behind Stan and Dick. All was forgotten, and they had resumed their macho banter. Stan was replying to Dick's question about summer plans.

"I'm doing as little as possible this summer. Fishing trip to Canada, a lot of golf, you know!"

"Good for you. You deserve it! You gonna use that graphite Shakespeare you bought?"

They were just two good guys talking about fishing.

"Guess I know what summer holds for me," Barbara thought. "A lot of Jim Benson and no extra pay for it. What a bitch!

My broken heart

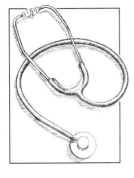

"How can you mend a broken heart?" asked the BeeGees in their '60s hit. It wasn't a particular favorite of mine, but was one of those song lyrics that, heard often enough, lurk in the recesses of your brain and pop out at unexpected times. That very thing happened to me while I was sitting in one of Dr. Mary Ann Anderson's Main Street Clinic examination rooms on a sultry July day in 2008.

Dr. Mary Ann and I are friends, which sometimes makes the doctor/patient relationship a little blurry. For instance, she can tell me that I must lose weight and in the ensuing discussion of what tactics to use in attaining that goal, we are suddenly talking baking and trading recipes. It just happens! "My new sweet roll recipe uses honey, and I'm not sure I like it as well as brown sugar," she confided, as we concluded our discussion of carbohydrates.

But just as I acknowledge her expertise in the culinary arts, I trust in and rely on her medical expertise. She knows my body almost better than I do, and can be relied upon for straight talk and a no nonsense approach to treatment. "I'm often dizzy, out of breath, and sometimes feel as if I might faint," I complained. She ordered an EKG test, which resulted in her diagnosis of atrial fibrillation, which meant that I had an irregular heartbeat, something that's fairly common but, in my case, was causing me to experience dangerous bouts of dizziness. I didn't understand then all the ramifications of the diagnosis, but did come immediately to the realization that, unlike the song lyrics, it was going to take something considerably more complicated than a romantic sweetheart (unfortunately, a prescription for this was not an option) to mend my broken heart.

My doc initiated several courses of action that afternoon: tests would be taken, blood pressure meds would be increased, and I would visit a Duluth (a nearby, larger medical facility) cardiologist within the next week. Problems were being addressed and I left with the assurance that all would be well.

I met with Dr. Albin at St. Mary's Hospital on another sultry July day. He was a stern-looking man in a suit who typed on a laptop constantly as we talked, setting down all his questions, my answers, and his recommendations. It was clear from the start that we wouldn't be exchanging salsa recipes at the end of the appointment.

He looked slightly surprised when I asked where he had received his training and somewhat proudly indulged me with the information that he had attended the University of Houston Cardiac and, at that time, had even met one of the great pioneers in open heart surgery, who was already a very old man. When my time had elapsed, he pressed a button to print a copy of the entire interview which involved basically the same meds my own doctor had prescribed but with one addition: In order to record all the irregular heartbeats, I would be fitted with a small electronic monitor which I would wear for 48 hours and mail back to him. It was this little robotic tattletale that told him my heart was not only beating erratically, but was stopping periodically for up to three seconds at a time. It can never be good when your heart stops, and, once again, it didn't take a cardiologist to tell me that. A female assistant called to give me this news, with his recommendation of a pacemaker.

Back to Dr. Mary Ann and a long discussion about the procedure. She explained that the meds I was taking to bring my blood pressure down probably caused the "power outages" in my heart and when a pacemaker was in place, it would immediately sense and correct the rhythm when this happened. She further explained that without the pacemaker allowing a regular, controlled rhythm, my heart would labor harder to beat and wear out faster.

"So, maybe I should just quit all the blood pressure meds, since they're causing the trouble.'

"Then your pressure goes up and you become a walking time bomb for a stroke or heart attack." It's a Catch 22 situation for sure or, less literary, what my mother used to say, "Damned if you do, and damned if you don't." So it was back to Duluth for this "damned" on the auspicious date of 9/11. Now if I were a superstitious person...

My daughter, son-in-law, and I arose in the middle of the night and drove in total darkness in order to be at the hospital for the procedure by check-in time at six-thirty. You know what happens next, right? You wait around until 11 o'clock for your turn at the knife.

I was awake for the whole procedure but felt no pain and didn't much care what was happening. I seem to remember a lot of yanking and pounding on my chest, but I'm not sure about that, because afterwards there didn't seem to be any trauma to that area, except for a gash where the pacemaker had been inserted. I got back to my bed feeling a little like I'd just had an out of body experience, which I actually had.

It's been three years since I started living with and depending on the little machine the size of a fifty cent piece.

I go for a tune up every three months to determine that the tiny battery is still charged. At that time their machine is connected to mine and, through the mysteries of medical science, I am able to see evidence of my heart beating away and the exact beat when the pacemaker takes over while the home team catches its breath.

In the meantime, Dr. Mary Ann and I continue to talk about my so far nonexistent weight loss and trade recipes or gardening tips. There goes that song again! I think they wired the BeeGees into the pacemaker. Is that legal?

The betrayal of Burton Bannister

A little more than kin, and less than kind

Shakespeare

The trees in this part of the woods are much bigger than they were when I was a kid. The trail is so overgrown; I can hardly tell if I'm even in the right area. But then I round a small hill, and there it is in a clearing: the huge oak with the tree house astride two thick, forked branches, the back wall leaning against the massive trunk. Even the boards nailed to the trunk as a makeshift ladder are intact, although some are missing or twisted vertically.

I start to climb, remembering how we used to do it on a dead run, and I slip and slide, clutching frantically for a hold on adjacent branches. My feet are too big now, and when I finally pull myself onto the branches holding the house, I'm breathing heavily, and I have to pause until the gasping slows. The house is amazingly solid: built to last by my Uncle Burton. I stick my head through the doorway. The initials we carved in the wall are still legible: ours primitive and uneven, while Uncle Burton's are almost like calligraphy with wide straight lines and curlicues on the rounded sides. Dead leaves and acorns have collected inside, but the structure is still sturdy and usable.

I arrange myself in the doorway of the tree house, my long, adult legs hanging over the supporting branches, and I sit for a while. It's pleasant with the light making changing patterns as it filters through the stirring leaves, and it's so quiet you can hear the sigh of the breeze in a nearby grove of pines or the scrape of branches that cross and lean on each other in their quest for the sky. The evergreens dispense spoors in the form of a yellow dust; and as the wind wafts this dust into the air and mixes it with sunlight, I'm enveloped in a peachy haze that possesses a dream quality to which I readily surrender, and I lean back and let my mind wander.

In retrospect I guess I had a pretty happy childhood. I'm not sure it was altogether happy for my parents, but with the self-absorbed recollection of an only son, I think I fared pretty well. So many of my memories are centered out here at the lake.

You see, my father was one of five brothers whose custom it was, with wives and children in tow, to spend Sundays at the family resort, Hickory Point, on Little Otter

Lake. To this day, a sunny, summer Sunday always takes me back to noon picnic dinners, long afternoons of play, with leave-taking extended into twilight so that all the kids could have at least one game of "Starlight, moonlight, I hope to see a ghost tonight." Selective memory has rendered these times idyllic, endless, and for the most part, rain free.

I can't remember having many Sundays rained out, but it must have happened and certainly did rain on one fateful Sunday afternoon which perpetrated the incident that changed our family dynamics forever, the incident that left a feeling of guilt in four male cousins. It was a guilt, which surfaced occasionally throughout our adult lives and had to be dealt with by rationalization, denial, and in some cases even therapy, forever hearing in dreams or thoughtful reminiscences the angry words of our paternal grandmother, Lovey Bannister.

"You boys broke our family!"

We called ourselves the BBs, which stood for Bannister Boys but metaphorically for the stinging ammunition of our BB guns. The group consisted of myself, Daryl Jr., Joe and Jake. Sometimes Daryl's little brother Peter tagged along and was a pain in the butt. Uncle Burton was the undisputed leader of this fearsome foursome and he pretty much directed the Sunday afternoon activities, always making sure we were having fun, were safe and that we included Peter when he chose to be with us.

The incident in question was the combined result of a sudden thunder storm, which ruined our outdoor play;

and a fire at our town's mill, which meant that my father and uncles left us unattended for a couple hours while they fought the fire, all five being members of the Otter Lake Volunteer Fire Department. When I think back on it, I don't know why it became such a tragedy: no one got hurt, except for upset stomachs, and nothing was broken... except for our family, that is.

"But you don't know the whole story, and it wasn't intentional!" At night I sometimes answer Grandma Lovey in a slow, garbled dream voice when visited by her apparition at my bedside. It was true! The BBs uncovered a mystery that rapidly grew beyond containment and was aggravated by the adults, whom we trusted to know better and make right. Adults who, unbeknownst to us, had secrets of their own which had to be kept at all cost, and who turned a simple incident into a competition about who had the most to lose.

Of the five Bannister men, first born was Uncle Arnold who, with his wife Aunt Beth, operated Hickory Point Resort. The Resort consisted of a main lodge decorated in a North Wisconsin theme: fieldstone fireplace, rustic furniture, and wall mounts of various fish and wildlife that had been unlucky enough to be within range of the fishermen and hunters who frequented the six cottages tucked into the surrounding woods.

The lodge was endlessly fascinating to us kids: there was the big metal cooler filled with ice, with a rollback top that cooled bottles of every kind of pop imaginable. What an extreme pleasure on a hot, July afternoon to plunge your arm up to the elbow in that ice water and select the flavor to slake the thirst that had built during the work-up softball game.

There was also a small store in the lodge which stocked toothbrushes, aspirin, Kleenex, candy bars, chips, and Cracker Jacks. We were allowed to select what we wanted, within reason and with permission. It was like heaven.

The apartment upstairs was Uncle Arnold and Aunt Beth's home, and we were cautioned that it was private and off limits unless invited, which we never were. They were the only Bannisters to not have children; and I heard my mother, Gwen, talking to her sisters-in-law and various friends about what she perceived was the result of this barren affliction. "She's a tough nut to crack," she'd say, "and Lord knows I've tried to be friendly. I think she enjoys having the children come on Sundays, which is why I make a point of going. Lord knows I'd just as soon be doing something else with my Sundays."

Mother always saw herself as being noble and self sacrificing and was also confident that the Lord knew of these virtues; but I knew she didn't have any other plans for Sundays. She enjoyed gossiping with the other wives, having dinner provided with only the contribution of a relish tray required, and having someone else responsible for her kids: my older sister, Karen, age 15, me, Max, age 13, and our baby sister, Melinda, age 3, "our little caboose."

Uncle Burton came next when Grandma Lovey decided to produce sons in alphabetical order. "Burton is definitely different," the sisters-in-law would whisper.

"He's a free spirit," his brothers concluded. But Grandma Lovey always stifled such discussions by pronouncing loudly,

"You boys are all my pride, but Burton is my joy!"

When Burton finished high school, he didn't know what he wanted to do, but definitely knew he didn't want to leave home. He'd always worked at the resort, same as all the boys, so it was easy to keep the status quo until his father's sudden death left him adrift. When Uncle Arnie proposed to take over Hickory Point, the deal was to include a job for Uncle Burton, which was eminently agreeable to Uncle Arnie and Aunt Beth. So he just stayed on, helping repair and paint the boats and helping Aunt Beth with the heavy cabin cleaning and redecorating during the winter months. In the summer there was plenty of general maintenance work and Burton was a friendly, talkative greeter for the guests, something neither Arnold nor Beth enjoyed.

When I went away to college and took my first psychology course, I recognized Uncle Burton instantly when I read about the Peter Pan syndrome. "That's it," I thought, "He just never grew up. He wasn't mentally challenged; he helped us with our math and corrected our English. At the same time he was charmingly childlike, pretending to sneak a bag of candy from the lodge which we'd take to our tree house and share, secretly leaving payment in the till, because he was exceedingly honest.

We all liked Uncle Burton best! Even my older sister and female cousin allowed as how he was neat, high praise from this finicky duo considering that the least disparaging title they assigned to us was snotball. But he complimented them on their outfits and never failed to notice a new hairdo. He even paid attention to the little kids, pushing them on the swings or drying their tears when they cried, which they constantly did. Who wouldn't like Uncle Burton? Imagine a playmate who displayed the physical and authoritative attributes of an adult but still climbed trees, played endless games of kick the can, and built a tree house exclusively for the BBs.

"He's just a big kid," Grandma Lovey said with a shake of her head. It was an oft repeated remark and gesture that when spoken by her was more with pride than regret. When it was the sisters-in-law speaking, it took on the feeling of a portent and made me uncomfortable and defensive on my uncle's behalf.

C stood for Charles who was my father and "a very successful lawyer," if you listened to my mother, and "Lord knows, a highly respected member of the community," which she was quick to remind me whenever there was cause to question or reprimand any of my behavior. I sometimes felt guilty that I didn't love him best, but he had grown up. Although I did come to respect and love him when I, myself, reached that much sought condition.

Uncle Daryl sold real estate and headed his own agency, Bannister Estates. He and Aunt Carrie moved older daughter

Carolyn, age 14, Daryl Jr., age 12, and Peter, age 9 from one fixer upper to another so often that even the family members needed a map to find them if the need arose. Uncle Daryl was pompous, always in a hurry, and constantly urging everyone in his vicinity to, make tracks.

Uncle Ed and Aunt Joan had the twins, Joe and Jake, age eleven. Mother said, "Those twins just sucked the life right out of Joan." I couldn't understand why they then went ahead and had Naomi, age eighteen months, but Mother said that sometimes accidents happened. I also didn't understand that, but lost interest in the whole subject.

Uncle Ed taught math at the high school and was the quietest of the uncles, or maybe he just seemed quiet because Aunt Joan talked all the time. She had many illnesses, all dating back to the birth of the twins. Mother said she was a hypochondriac which sounded really serious when I was thirteen years old.

The afternoon in question started out like every other Sunday. Four of the brothers, their wives and Grandma Lovey sat in lawn chairs on the deck. The kids, family and various visiting cabin dwellers, and Uncle Burton ran and screamed and ducked behind trees across the lawn and into the woods. The picnic table, spread with bowls and baskets of tempting salads, casseroles, and desserts, was just beyond the deck on the grass.

"This property would bring us all a pretty penny on today's market." Uncle Daryl had cornered Uncle Arnie as he refilled his plate at the picnic table. "People from the Cities are looking for businesses in the country or for a little, weekend getaway cabin. It's possible we could subdivide and make even more money if we made tracks in that direction."

"Where does that leave me and Beth, or Burton?" Uncle Arnold looked at his brother in disbelief.

"I'm just throwing this out there for discussion. Hell, you could retire and move wherever you want. I'm talking pretty penny here, just for your share."

"You boys quit your arguing! Nobody's selling Hickory Point! Not while I'm alive!"

Grandma Lovey bustled to the table, her hands making shooing motions in the air as if to disperse bad thoughts. Grandma Lovey, so named for the endearment she lavished on all her children and grandchildren, shared a small house on the resort with Burton. Her sons had built it just for her, and although she now knew little of what went on in the business and probably less of what occurred in the family, she reigned as a benevolent matriarch, bold in her belief that she was still in charge by virtue of being the lone survivor of her generation of the family.

As the story went, our great grandfather, Maxwell Bannister, came across the wooded property on the lake in the early '30s when he had come north to fish, seeking some respite from a grueling factory job in Milwaukee.

But his restful recreation was forgotten when he began to see what could be done with the land and knew from firsthand experience that there was a market in the cities for reasonable vacation places.

His original idea was for a fishing camp and he somehow talked a bank into giving him a loan, took the risk of quitting his job and moving his family to the site, and went about building small, primitive cabins where city slickers could experience the joys of roughing it in the northwoods. His inventory was simple: a few rowboats, some fishing equipment, and cast iron pans for frying fish. He was a tireless worker, and also built the original lodge as his family's home. And he was successful. The lake gained a reputation for good fishing, and the Camp provided a comfortable living for the Bannister family.

However, gradually the needs of the vacationing population changed. Men who frequented the Camp soon started bringing their wives and children with them to enjoy the glorious northwoods only to find that their wives wanted indoor plumbing and activities for the children and themselves while the men fished. Business waned just before World War II and all but disappeared during that long conflict.

Then came 1945 and the war-weary country came alive with the possibilities of the post-war era. My Grandpa Bob was mustered out of the army after serving on the European Theater of Operations and with his new wife, Vera (eventually to be Lovey) took over the business, turning the unglamorous Fishing Camp into Hickory Point Resort. They were able to get GI loans and with savings they had accrued during the war when life was on hold, they began to modernize the cabins, dredge the lake for a swimming beach, expand the lodge, invest in a few canoes and outboard motors, and put up play equipment. The place took off like a rocket, and so it continued to prosper until our day, now with Uncle Arnold and Aunt Beth at the helm.

On this particular Sunday afternoon, a spirited game of hide and seek seemed to be amusing the spectators as much as the players. Uncle Burton was running full out for home plate while several nephews were attempting to catch him before he reached safety. "Run Burton!" Uncle Ed impulsively shouted before catching himself and laughing apologetically as he shook his head. The restrained envy of the three, seated uncles was palpable: each secretly wished he could once again cavort with abandon like a child, or like their brother Burton.

"I didn't say we should do it, I just thought we could discuss it like adults." Uncle Daryl had drawn his chair close to my Dad and was talking in low tones.

"I know, I know, but you must understand how Arnie feels. It's his career, like we have law and real estate. How'd you like it if I suggested you close your agency and move away?"

"Well it's not at all the same. I own my agency. Hickory Point belongs to us five Bannister brothers; it's right in Lovey's will. Maybe I'd like to do something different with my share, aside from spending every Sunday out here, that is. What's in this arrangement for us?"

"Now I don't think you mean that! You've gotta take into consideration all the improvements Arnie's made with his own money. You also gotta remember that he takes care of Lovey and Burton. They're our family. We gotta watch out for each other." Dad had adopted a tone of camaraderie and nudged Uncle Daryl with his shoulder, as if the two of them were the watchdogs of the family.

"Oh, I'm well aware that he's put money into the resort, but he was given the land and a damn good start. We had to build our own lives, with no help from the old man I might add."

"Come on Daryl, we're all doing okay. Why rock the boat? We're all in the prime of life. Time enough to talk about selling and shares when we're old geezers." He clapped Daryl on the back and rose to fill his coffee cup from the thermos on the table.

Uncle Ed also rose and stood behind Dad, as if waiting in line. He too spoke quietly and out of earshot of the group on the deck. He and Dad walked together across the lawn, holding their coffee cups and talking privately.

About that time, Mother jumped up as Uncle Burton approached her, carrying a crying Melinda and holding her skinned knee away from his chest, so it wouldn't be irritated by rubbing against his shirt,

"Blood, Mommy," she wailed.

"Good Lord!" my mother answered.

All of a sudden it became darker as a large, black cloud bank moved rapidly over the lake and covered the sun. Everyone looked at the sky. A brisk wind came up and began blowing napkins and paper plates around the yard, tipping lawn chairs and whisking waxed paper covers off picnic dishes. The aunts rushed to clear away the dinner, and all the kids were pressed into service carrying dishes and folding lawn chairs.

Several guests were caught on the lake and were now hurrying to shore. Uncle Arnie helped them beach their boats while Uncle Burton secured the oars and cushions, making several trips to the boathouse for storage.

Just as rain began to fall, slanted sideways by the wind, we were inside the lodge in a jumble of talking and crying and adults barking orders, but a lull descended on the unruly aggregation when the phone rang and we could hear Uncle Arnie talking hurriedly to someone. "They're all here," he said. "We'll be right over." He hung up the phone and signaled for quiet. "The warehouse at the mill is on fire. They need everyone down there to keep it from spreading to other buildings." He started for the door, then remembered, "Somebody call Burton," he yelled back, "He's out at the boathouse."

"Hell, I've got a lot of real estate in that area," Uncle Daryl said as he located his car keys and headed for the door.

"We can all go together in my van," my Dad offered.

"What about us?" my Mother tugged at his sleeve as he was about to leave.

"Just stay here until we get back. The storm will blow over soon and you can all go outside again."

"Men always get to go and leave us with all this." Mother swept her arms wide encompassing the milling crowd of children and attending women. The BBs were taunting the teenage girls who, in turn, were yelling threats and calling us disgusting names; Peter was afraid of thunder and cringed in the corner whenever it clapped and the little girls, Melinda and Naomi, cried.

I was in the process of executing a double nose-thumb when Aunt Beth grabbed me and Daryl Jr. (usually called just Junior) by each an upper arm and halted our scenario. She was strong and held us immobile while she calmly said; "You boys go play out on the screened porch until you can behave with other people."

I felt momentarily ashamed. Aunt Beth was always good to us. She cooked most of the food at the Sunday dinners and remembered our favorite dishes. She packed brownies and cupcakes for us to take home and sometimes smiled and tousled our hair when we were leave taking. We thought she was a good egg.

We were chastened and marched toward the porch slowly until Joe started to laugh. That was the release we needed, and we ran for the door, bursting onto a somewhat wet and uninviting venue. We all fleetingly wondered what we were going to do for amusement out there, when a noise drew my eye to the door of the boathouse flapping wildly in the wind, its padlock hanging open on the hasp. In his hurry to get to the fire, Uncle Burton had forgotten to lock the door when he had finished stowing the boat gear.

"Hey," I cried, "Let's go play in the boathouse." Now, the boathouse was another place on the resort that was off limits to everyone but Uncle Burton and Uncle Arnie and was kept locked at all times, but the unusual circumstance of the storm and the temptation of the unlocked door seemed to grant permission to the four of us who were desperate to save the day.

We ducked our heads into our shoulders and ran in the rain from the porch. Thunder rolled overhead and lightning streaked across the lake as we entered the dim space and adjusted our eyes to the lack of light. Oars, ropes, anchors, motors, and tarps were piled against one wall, orderly and easily accessible. However, the rest of the space was set up like a bedroom; a bed with sheets and a comforter occupied a corner. There was a little round table with a lamp, a radio and five chairs. A cupboard stood against another wall with doors held shut by a simple hook and eye. It was as if we had stumbled into the story of Goldilocks and The Three Bears, only there were five chairs.

"Neat," said Jake as we fanned out exploring these unfamiliar surroundings. Joe jumped on the bed, dislodging a magazine called *Jugs* from under the pillow, a title and term that was unfamiliar to us. We crowded around him as he turned the pages from one naked lady to another, each one with bigger breasts than the one before.

Joe lay back on the pillow with his hands behind his head. I flicked the switch on the lamp, and a cozy light glowed in the room. We looked through the magazine again, now enhanced by the soft, golden light of the lamp. As the rain drummed on the metal roof of the boathouse, we spent a long time, silently perusing the copy of *Jugs*, selecting and arguing over our favorite ladies and poses.

"I wonder what's in the cupboard," Jake brought us back to earth as he lifted the hook and swung the doors open, and here was the biggest surprise of all. Bottles of wine, whiskey, and vodka were in the front row, with various bottles of exotic liquors in back. There were also appropriate glasses and tins of nuts and other salty accompaniments for cocktails.

"I wonder who this is for. Uncle Arnie and Uncle Burton don't drink, and they're the only ones who have keys to this place," I said. We had inadvertently discovered a mystery that I knew had to be solved. Junior selected a syrupy looking red liquid in a fancy bottle and poured a small amount in a glass. We all watched with baited breath as he took the first sip.

"It's pretty good," he announced as he poured a little

more and sat down importantly at the table, swirling the liquid around in the glass and holding it out appreciatively. The twins scrambled to select a drink of their own, and I tipped the whiskey bottle and took a long draught, showing off for the younger boys. I had no idea anything could taste so awful, and I sputtered and shook until warmth spread down my throat and into my stomach. Next I tried a green liquid that tasted of peppermint, which went down much easier. And so it went. Someone turned on the radio, and we sat round the table, talking and laughing together much like our fathers would at a bar. It was ever thus: the more we drank the rowdier we became, and soon we forgot all about being cautious and quiet. Junior started using the bed as a trampoline and from the sheets, unearthed a pair of lace panties, which he proceeded to fit on his head like a cap. It must have been quite a scene when the door opened suddenly.

"What are you guys doing in here?" Uncle Burton was at the open door with a look on his face we had never seen before. It was like shock, fear, and anger all at once, and he pulled each one of us in turn by one arm and all but flung us out the door into the rain that was still falling steadily. He had never been mad at us before and that along with the shock of the cold rain rendered us immediately sober and frightened.

I tried to explain. "We came out to close the door that was flapping, and we decided to investigate," I started, "We didn't mean anything." Uncle Burton tried to quickly lock the door, but by then aunts and uncles came running in the rain, just as Junior leaned over and vomited in the grass. There were sounds of surprise and disgust from the aunts as they pushed by Uncle Burton and peered into the boathouse at the rumpled bed and the table littered with glasses and bottles and the copy of *Jugs*, now wrinkled and sticky with spilled liqueurs.

"This is degenerate!"

"Who uses this?"

"What is the meaning of this?" Aunt Joan pulled the panties from Junior's head and held them up. "Someone is bringing women in here."

Uncle Burton stood by the open door with his head bowed and his hands hanging useless at his sides. As the aunts investigated the space, he looked from one to the other of his brothers with apologetic eyes, like a dog who knows he's done wrong but needs to be forgiven.

"You must have known about this, Arnie!" My Mother was challenging him as he stepped forward to replace the padlock and snap it shut. The other brothers seemed almost to cower in the background as Uncle Arnie confronted the imposing presence of my Mother, leaning directly into her face.

"Of course I knew about it. I know everything that goes on at Hickory Point. It's a private space and your boys should have respected that. It's nobody's business."

"But who uses it for drinking and Lord knows what?"

"That doesn't concern you."

"It concerns me when my son is dragged into this degradation!"

"Nobody dragged him."

It was at this point that my Father took charge. "Everyone calm down," he shouted. "Gwen, you and Carrie and Joan pack up and get the kids in the car. We'll be with you shortly." Mother started to protest, but surprisingly, she thought better of it and followed the others to the lodge. I tried to stay for the brothers' discussion, but Mother pushed me ahead of her.

"You're one of the kids, mister!" she informed me.

Aside from my swirling equilibrium and nausea on the ride home, I was further frustrated at not being able to hear the whispered but heated argument that raged between my parents in the front seat. I was only able to put together the gist of the explanation my Father offered.

"For God's sake, Gwen, he's a grown man! How'd you like to work for your brother your whole life and live with and take care of Lovey? That was his private space and the only place he could go to relax and feel like a man."

"Act like a pervert, you mean! Lord knows if he limited his manly vices to the boathouse. Maybe he taught the boys a few things out in that tree house in the woods. When I think of how he carried my baby around, it makes me sick, and more than once I've thought he paid a little too much attention to the older girls." Mother was warming to her subject, as she often did, and giving herself great instincts in hind sight that had never before occurred to her.

"Burton's a good guy," my Dad defended, "he loves all those kids and would never do anything to hurt them. You know yourself how he always tells them not to drink or smoke and to listen in school. He'd give them money rewards for good report cards, for Christ's sake!"

"There's no need to swear," Mother hissed. "And that makes it doubly bad, being a hypocrite. He was just gaining their confidence."

"To what end? What was in it for him?"

"Companionship! To do his filthy things; oh, I don't know!"

Evidently, according the other three BBs, much the same arguments took place that afternoon in Uncle Daryl's and Uncle Ed's cars. The brothers all defended Uncle Burton but the sisters-in-law formed a formidable alliance that, for some reason unknown to us kids, their husbands were unwilling to oppose. Did that mean that Uncle Burton was really guilty, and his brothers' silence was tacit admittance? Maybe he was a pervert after all! When the BBs had a chance to talk together, we all began to remember times when he had done or said some questionable things.

I even remember feeling I had been betrayed when I began to believe, through constant repetition, my Mother's version of what went on "out at the lake." But maybe she provided me with an easy way to pass the blame rather than to feel guilty about having exposed my favorite uncle. We were just kids, and for us loyalties changed on an hourly basis over situations as trite as who had money for after school treats to things as serious as physically aligning ourselves with a side in schoolyard brawls. Anyway, whatever the cause, we all began to see Uncle Burton in a different light.

The first Sunday gathering after the incident was an awkward one. We were given the new rules before arrival at Hickory Point: the tree house was now off limits; all games and playing with Uncle Burton had to take place on the front lawn with the parents watching from the deck; and we weren't to accept treats or presents from Uncle Burton. Of course the afternoon was a disaster. We were all bored and ended up sitting around the deck bugging our parents to go home. None of them had realized how much Burton cared for and entertained the offspring, allowing the adults a pleasant break.

It was particularly heartbreaking to watch Uncle Burton who seemed to be unaware that he had been caste in the role of the pariah. "You guys want to get some pop and go down to the tree house?" We shook our heads, no one bothering to explain why. Then he offered to push Melinda on the swing and put out his hand. But as she reached for him, Mother whisked her onto her lap and turned her back on her brother-in-law. Melinda cried.

Uncle Arnie seemed tense with suppressed anger, and talked little and ate next to nothing from the picnic table. We all left early, much to Grandma Lovey's dismay.

"What's wrong with all of you?" she asked loudly as we packed up to leave.

"Everyone's upset about what happened last Sunday," my Dad tried to explain.

"What happened last Sunday?" She evidently hadn't absorbed any of the undercurrents of that afternoon. "There was the storm and the fire. Why are you all mad at each other?" Simply put like that, the whole ruckus seemed unnecessary. and in retrospect, it could have been a time for rational thought.

"The boys made a mess and caused hard feelings," Dad said.

"Boys always make messes, but the real messes happen when the adults try to take up for them." For once, Grandma Lovey was offering real advice, gleaned from years of raising boys and dealing with people. But everyone was in the habit of not listening to her, and her opinion went unheard and unconsidered.

After that, the Sunday picnics became an endurance test for everyone. Gradually Uncle Burton quit trying to interact with any of the kids. Then he quit making an appearance at the picnics altogether, sometimes just coming to fix a plate and sit next to Grandma Lovey in a lawn chair (obviously at her request) until he excused himself formally on the pretext of some errand. My Dad and uncles looked at him with pity but didn't urge him to stay.

The BBs wondered if he spent those afternoons at his retreat in the boathouse. "Ill bet he's got a new *Jugs,* Junior said somewhat longingly.

"Nah," Jake said, "he's probably got the woman who fits those panties in there."

"Let's find out," I suggested boldly. And so we snuck away while the women were in the kitchen and the men were deep in conversation. We ambled off into the woods, and then circled back around to the boathouse, creeping low as we'd seen it done in the movies. Slowly we raised our heads to look through the one window. As our eyes adjusted to the gloomy interior, we made out the familiar objects: bed, cupboard, table. Then a slight movement caused us to focus on one of the chairs. A small figure, certainly not Uncle Burton, sat at the table, head bent with fingers encircling a glass. The whiskey bottle stood in close proximity, as if the availability of a refill was crucial.

"Maxwell!" Mother's voice shattered the secrecy of the mission, and we scrambled to creep away unnoticed, circle back, and re-enter the lawn area from a different direction.

"What?" I yelled with irritation, wanting to convey my disgust at having been disturbed on a simple walk. "Can't we do anything any more?" Even at that age I was aware that the best defense was an offense.

"That sure wasn't Uncle Burton in there," Jake whispered

as we strolled across the lawn, "it looked like a woman."
Then I had another idea and motioned the BBs to stay put
as I hurried to the kitchen. The women and girls were
dishing up desserts. All that is, except Aunt Beth

"Where's Aunt Beth?"

"Who wants to know?" Mother was still smarting from
our previous encounter. "She felt a headache and went
upstairs for a little lie-down. What's it to you, mister?"

"I just wondered if she still had that old cat that was
hanging around," I improvised.

"Since when have you been an animal lover, dirtwad,"
my sister countered. I put thumb and forefinger in the whip-
ped cream bowl, flicked a big blob of cream in her face
and ran from the room. "Mother, he got cream on my new
blouse," she yelled.

"Well, I'm afraid you asked for that one," Mother said.

"It's Aunt Beth," I informed the waiting BBs, and we all
sat down on a bench by the lake to absorb this new mystery.

"Is Aunt Beth still sick?" I asked casually as we packed
the picnic basket into the trunk of the car and crawled into
our accustomed places.

"What's all this concern with Aunt Beth?" Mother asked,
and Dad flashed me a questioning look.

"Oh, nothing. You just said she had a headache, and she
wasn't there to say goodbye."

"What a weirdo!" my sister spit out. I kicked her foot
hard, and she yelled, and Mother reached back to administer

a communal slap, which went awry as we both sucked in our bodies and plastered ourselves against the back seat. By that time everyone forgot to question me further.

That fall I entered Otter Lake High School and put aside all childish pursuits like tree houses, the BBs, and the boat house mystery for basketball and the big, blue eyes of Sally Bergval. It turned out I was pretty good at the sport and actually made it onto the varsity team, although I spent a lot of time riding the pine. With Sally, on the other hand, I was in the game from the beginning, which was almost more responsibility than I could handle.

Family dynamics changed too. Although my sister and cousin, Carolyn, were ahead of me in school, they were forced to afford me a grudging respect, since I was on the team with a number of boys they wished to impress. Even Mother and Dad gave me special treatment once in awhile and showed up at all the games on the off chance I'd play. I was heady with my minimal success, and Hickory Point Resort was all but forgotten.

We didn't go out there much any more. Dad went out to visit every week, however, and sometimes Mom and Melinda would go along. Then, in the spring of my sophomore year, Grandma Lovey had a stroke and died after lingering for a couple weeks in a vegetative state. "Lord knows it was a blessing," my Mother concluded.

Aunt Beth fixed a meal for after the funeral and the whole family, plus friends and acquaintances, gathered in the lodge. It was rather surreal being in familiar surroundings but also being aware that everything and everyone had changed.

Aunt Beth exhibited the greatest physical change: she was painfully thin, with pronounced cheekbones and protruding hipbones. She had gotten very gray and looked tired. She smiled and hugged me, which was uncharacteristic of her, and elicited feelings from me, which I had never before felt. I hugged her tightly and saw her eyes fill with tears.

Uncle Burton looked smaller than I'd remembered, but maybe it was because I'd grown bigger. He was certainly less boisterous and shook my hand formally and asked about basketball, even singling out games when I had played, leading me to believe he had been among the spectators. Maybe he displayed his grief more than his brothers, but I'd noticed during the funeral that he was the one son who had to wipe away tears.

Only the two little girls were kids now and ran around the adults' legs laughing and screaming in spite of the somber occasion. Groups of people balanced their plates and talked quietly, and the oft-repeated phrase rose above the muted conversation of the crowd: "It was a blessing."

When only the Bannister family remained, the coffee cups were filled and for the first time in a long while, everyone sat together around the big, fieldstone fireplace. Spring in Northern Wisconsin is always an elusive season, and it was a raw, windy day with the large picture window revealing the whitecaps and churning waves of an angry looking Little Otter Lake. Uncle Arnie knelt in front of the fire, occasionally stirring it with a poker and adding more logs. I thought it was a comfortable time and a healing for the bad feelings that had persisted. Grandma Lovey would have approved. Too bad we couldn't have come together while she still lived.

I was surprised when Dad leaned forward and called the family to attention. I thought he was going to comment on the family solidarity. I had forgotten that death sometimes meant the disbursement of personal belongings. Because Lovey had exerted so little influence for so long, I had forgotten that she still owned Hickory Point, and I was suddenly aware that others in the crowd had not forgotten; Uncle Daryl and Uncle Ed imperceptibly leaned forward in their chairs.

"As you all know, I have handled Lovey's legal affairs ever since I became a lawyer, not that there was that much to do. Now that she has passed on, the only thing left is to execute the terms of her will." He paused, and the crowd coughed, shifted positions, and drank from their cups. "Many of you saw the will years ago when it was drafted at the time of our father's death. What you don't know is that Lovey came to me several months ago and drafted a new will, which, of course, takes precedence over the original. It was also her wish at the time that no one in the family know about the new will, and I was honor bound by the code of my profession to respect her wishes. I will now read the legal will of Vera Eliza Bannister, trusting that you will all understand her reasons for change and my reasons for confidentiality."

Surprise registered on everyone's face, even Mother's. I knew Dad would hear about this failure to share with his wife as a result of the revelation. Everyone kept quiet, however, eager to hear the new will. Dad read loudly and with great deliberation, including and pronouncing every legal term distinctly, as if to impress everyone with the binding obligations of the document. What became clear out of the whereas and inasmuch language was that Grandma Lovey had left Hickory Point Resort to her sons Arnold and Burton equally and had, "remained confident that they would continue to successfully operate the resort; and that her other sons would continue to prosper in their chosen professions."

There was a moment of shocked silence when chins dropped and looks were exchanged, then everyone started talking at once. Uncle Daryl rose from his chair and pointed at Dad with a raised arm.

"Fuck your oath of confidentiality," Uncle Daryl all but shouted. "You knew I was over extending myself in anticipation of an inheritance, you could have given me a heads up on this, brother."

"I advised you not to overinvest. That was all I could do."

"Why would our own Mother turn her back on us?" Uncle Ed seemed to be talking to himself, then suddenly turned the question to Dad, who stood again and signaled for quiet.

"She explained to me that she felt the three of us – me, Daryl, and Ed – had been given college educations in our chosen careers; whereas Arnie and Burton had stayed with and invested their time in the Resort. Hickory Point was near and dear to Lovey's heart. She and Dad made it what it is today and she wanted it to remain in the family for generations. We all thought she didn't know what was going on behind her back, but she knew you were talking about selling." Here, he turned to Uncle Daryl, then back to the group. "She knew we were making comfortable livings on our own. She also expressed to me that although she wasn't exactly sure what had happened, she knew we were blackballing Burton for some unknown transgression, and she felt that, as we'd done so many times when we were children, we were using him as a scapegoat. She did what she could for him by investing him with some authority."

"Don't tell me he didn't go crying to Mama!" Uncle Daryl was brutal with his sarcasm.

"No one told her anything," Dad insisted. "She even asked me what had happened and I stuck to the story."

"Lord knows," Mother said, "no one wanted her to know what Burton was up to. It would have killed her."

"But what did I do?" Uncle Burton stood with his palms turned up and hands spread.

"Don't play dumb with us," Aunt Carrie shouted. "It's one thing to keep it from your mother, but we all know the truth."

"Shut up, Carrie!" Uncle Daryl motioned her down.

"I think I might faint," Aunt Joan announced in a voice strong enough to be heard above what had turned into an angry mob.

"Good Lord!" Mother rolled her eyes heavenward.

Uncle Arnold stood, still clutching the poker in one hand. "I don't think there can be any more rational discussion here today. We all need to get our heads around this development and realize the implications for all of us. I think everyone should go home."

"Absolutely right," my Dad agreed.

"You haven't heard the last of this," Uncle Daryl spoke to Uncle Arnold. "I may not have taken a law degree, but I know that wills can be contested. Make tracks!" he advised his family as they executed a disorganized retreat.

Abruptly the coats were distributed and doors were slammed. Our family stayed until last. "He'll get over it," Dad said to Uncle Arnold. "You know how he blows up and gets it out of his system."

I felt too confused to fight with Karen on the way home, and Melinda had mercifully fallen asleep in her car seat. Mother and Dad exchanged just a few words in the front seat.

"Leave it to that old woman to throw her weight around even from the grave." Mother was adjusting her coat, but looked up suddenly at the tone of Dad's response to her comment.

"Don't talk about my mother that way! I, for one, think

she showed a great deal of courage, more than any of us men have. She was the only one who did the right thing."

Even in the dim interior of the car I could see the tears welling in Dad's eyes as, for the first and only time I'd ever heard, he spoke sharply to Mother.

Well, Uncle Daryl contested the will, but lost. From what I gathered, despite being excluded from adult conversations and not being that interested anyway, Uncle Daryl was forced to sell a great deal of real estate he had bought on the off chance that the City of Otter Lake would expand in certain directions. He and Aunt Carrie moved to another fixer-upper and the family didn't see much of them after all the litigation was over.

Uncle Ed was my math teacher but kept any contact on a professional level and almost seemed embarrassed and tongue-tied if we found ourselves alone together. The summer before my junior year, Dad said Uncle Ed had found a better teaching position down state and would be leaving Otter Lake High School. I felt bad about the twins leaving, as the BBs had tried to stay somewhat together at school, even though we were in different grades.

Everything about the uncles and their families was shrouded in an air of mystery. If I asked questions, I was given condescending answers that translated into, "You're too young to know." Could they all possibly still be smarting over the boathouse incident? The older I grew, the more I sensed the rift had underlying causes; but I was young and self centered, and stored the Bannister family dysfunction deep in my subconscious while I dealt with more important things, like basketball, girls, and college.

Then just before Christmas, Aunt Beth died and I was shocked into adulthood for a short time. I had been genuinely fond of her and still remembered how she had hugged me when Grandma Lovey died. I felt sorrow and guilt that I hadn't seen her more often or paid more attention to her. I felt anger when I learned that she had been surviving with cancer for some time and no one had told me she was sick. "We didn't want you to worry about such things when you're so young," Dad had explained.

"I should have been told," I cried. "I'm not a child, you know!" But I was still a child, and soon Aunt Beth and the funeral faded into the background and were replaced with maybe not more important, but certainly more current concerns.

I took to going out to Hickory Point with Dad occasionally, and even the casual observer could tell that Uncle Arnie and Uncle Burton were going through the motions of day-to-day living like lost souls. That quiet, mousey woman had breathed life into them and given them a reason to work, play, laugh, cry, and enjoy – to exist. They hired Mrs. McCulloch, who lived down the road, to clean the cabins and handle reservations, the check-in and out business, and clerk in the little store.

Then more and more, Peter, Uncle Daryl's youngest son, started appearing behind the counter or raking the yard, or cleaning boats. "He came out himself and asked for a job," I heard Uncle Arnie tell Dad. "I'm sure Daryl knows. He drives him out sometimes, but I haven't heard a word from him. He's a good little worker, I'll tell you that."

Even I noticed a difference in the place when Peter was there. Gradually it came back to life. I'm now ashamed to admit that Peter had always been the butt of the BB's jokes and ridicule when we were forced to include him, but for him that experience had translated into a deeper understanding of and appreciation for Uncle Burton and I felt a pang of envy when I saw them together and realized that they were the best of friends, laughing and roughhousing the way brothers or a close father and son would. After all, he had been my favorite Uncle first, before the boathouse, that is.

I came home little during college, even finding summer work in another town. My decision to go to law school, however, met with great approval from my parents and engendered an amount of pride. A couple times I heard Mother brag to her friends, "I expect he'll be going into his father's firm in town."

"That will never happen," I thought to myself; but since I've been low man at a firm in my college town for several years after law school, I'm beginning to look favorably at my Dad's offer to join him. My future wife, Rita Taylor, is enthusiastic about living in Otter Lake, and I began to look back at my childhood and at my parent's life in a small town and allowed as how it could be pretty good.

Dad's voice roused me from my extended reverie as he called from the woods beyond the clearing. "Over here, Dad," I answered, "I'm in the treehouse." I watched him approach the tree and noticed for the first time his white hair and cautious gait. I climbed down the ladder, slipping and sliding to the ground.

"I've got to sit down a little while," he said sounding winded. We found a fairly solid birch log in the woods, its parchment bark still intact but curled and frayed.

I thought it the perfect time to at last formally become an adult to my father, and get answers to some of the questions I had once again formulated as I sat in the tree house.

"Dad, what is the background of that incident in the boathouse that sort of broke up the family? I think I'm finally old enough to know." I laughed as I spoke to lighten the mood.

"What do you want to know?" Suddenly he looked defeated and very sad.

"Who used that place? Was it really Uncle Burton's sort of man cave?' Did he have girl friends? What was all the fuss about?"

"Max, I have few regrets in my life; but the betrayal of Burton over that boathouse is to this day my number one regret, or should I call it a sin. I've thought to set you straight on the subject many times over the years, but could never bear to have you think badly of me. We let our brother down to save our own skins because we thought he had nothing to lose. It turned out that everyone has something to lose, even Burton, and for him it was us." Dad shifted his weight on the log and began.

"It started out innocent enough. Beth didn't want liquor in the lodge for fear it would encourage drunken guests and all that entailed for them as owners, but she didn't object to Arnie having an occasional drink, so he took to keeping a bottle in the boathouse and even moved in a little refrigerator for beer. Burton knew about it but didn't care for the taste of alcohol, so he paid no attention. On many a Sunday afternoon when the women were gossiping and Burton was playing with the kids, the men would retire to the boathouse on the pretext of viewing some motor or piece of equipment that needed repair or was new. We'd stand around and enjoy a beer or pour a shot of whiskey into our bottles of pop we'd brought from the lodge. It was a good time among brothers.

"We got tired of leaning on sawhorses or against the wall, and Arnie brought in an old table and five chairs to make our drinking time more comfortable. Next came the cupboard, ordered from and fashioned by Burton with his handy carpenter skills. I remember the Sunday he installed it, so proud when we all thanked him and admired it."

"I don't remember discussing the addition of the bed. When it appeared, Daryl said he'd replaced a bed at his house and wanted to get rid of this one. He thought it might be useful for something. The same was said of the radio and lamp. Then liquors and glasses began to appear in the cupboard."

"One Sunday I noticed a porno magazine on the bed and looked quizzically at Arnie. He said that Daryl had taken to coming out at odd times on some occasions and resting, reading, and drinking in the boathouse. Sometimes he'd bring guests. He allowed as how Daryl had a very stressful life and needed a getaway. "So I give him the key when he wants." I nodded in agreement.

"And what about the lace panties?" I seemed relentless even to myself.

"That was the worst part. It wasn't until the day of the storm and fire that I learned that Ed had been having an affair with a colleague of his from the high school. That very afternoon he'd talked to me privately, as his lawyer, about getting a divorce from Joan, so he could marry this other teacher. We talked about his children, one a mere baby, and his teaching job at the high school. I sympathized with his feelings, but I reminded him of his commitment to his family. "It will be a scandal," I told him, "for your mother, brothers, wife, children, not to mention the damage to your friend's family and job." I asked him where they rendezvoused, hoping that he hadn't been observed by anyone, and he told me he got the boathouse key from Burton on certain nights, although Burton had no knowledge of her or what went on in the boathouse."

"Well, when you boys got into the boathouse, the cat

was out of the bag, so to speak; and at the hasty meeting Daryl said it would go very bad for his marriage if Carrie found out about his retreat, and Ed cried as he confessed his indiscretions to his brothers and begged them to cover for him. Daryl suggested that they say it was Burton's retreat since he was the only one unmarried. Both Arnie and I were against this plan but Burton, because he really didn't understand the extent of what had gone on in the boathouse and actually thought the incident was his fault for leaving the door unlocked, seemed eager to assume the blame in order to get back in the good graces of his brothers.

"It's my fault. I left the door open," he kept repeating. I honestly thought the whole thing would blow over, but the women couldn't forget about the lace panties and magazine and convinced themselves that Burton was corrupting their families and probably had been for some time."

Dad sat on the log hugging his knees and looking straight ahead, as he waited for my comments. "Wow," I said, "that was pretty serious for Uncle Ed. He took no further action on divorce, huh? Which teacher was his lover," a totally selfish question, but I wanted to know.

"The lady was a phy ed teacher, Mrs. Eaton. Her husband was transferred out of Otter Lake, and to my knowledge, she left town without ever considering a divorce or a life with Ed."

I knew Mrs. Eaton, not well because she taught girl's phy ed, but she was glamorous in an older woman sort of way and was very friendly and happy. In short, she was the exact opposite of Aunt Joan.

"Poor Uncle Ed," I said, "But why didn't you all defend Uncle Burton to your wives?"

"We tried, but we couldn't tell them the whole truth." Dad turned his face to look me in the eye. "If we told the truth, Joan would have divorced Ed, or had a breakdown, or both. Maybe Carrie would have done the same to Daryl. That would have been a scandal for the whole family. Lovey was right. We made Burton the scapegoat."

So the brothers had made a gentlemen's' club out of the boathouse, each one for his own purpose. I didn't add to Dad's obvious guilt by suggesting that the Bannister brothers had not only made a scapegoat of Burton but also of their sons, the BBs, who for years had harbored the impression that they had broken the family," as Lovey had accused.

Dad shook his head in regret and as a gesture of finality. "We'd best hurry," he said, "We're supposed to be there by six-thirty." The sun was high in the sky. It was a hot day in August and perspiration beaded on Dad's forehead as a result of the humid air, or possibly it was due to the painful admission he had just made. As we walked faster towards Hickory Point Resort and the flat, unmoving surface of Little Otter Lake, I put my arm around Dad's shoulders to assure him that I still loved and respected him

When we entered, Arnie came to us immediately and shook my hand and held Dad in an awkward embrace. His eyes were red rimmed from crying and his lips trembled when he spoke. "Hell of a hot day," he commented, and we both agreed. A very adult Peter came next, and I was

THE CLOUD FACTORY

surprised at his poise and friendliness, even though you could tell he had been crying too. Mrs. McCulloch had prepared a supper and the brothers and their extended families filled their plates from the dining room table and found spaces around the air-conditioned lodge to sit and eat quietly.

"Peter has turned into quite a self-assured young man," I said, feeling curiously old and condescending. Dad leaned toward me to whisper something, but we were drawn into other conversations until suddenly we heard Mother's voice,

"Good Lord, Melinda!" All eyes followed hers to the door where eleven-year-old Melinda and ten-year-old Naomi stood giggling. Although fully clothed, they were dripping mud and water.

"We fell in the lake," they explained in chorus, and I detected the gleam in their eyes and remembered using the same excuse when the BBs would start roughhousing on the dock and end up in the water. Some things never change, I thought happily.

There was a thunderstorm that night, dissipating the humid heat and the next day dawned bright and cool. I started for the church early. I had a stop to make before the service, but got there just as the first attendees were filing in. As was the old fashioned custom, the casket was open in the vestibule so that those who hadn't attended the viewing the night before could have one last chance to say their goodbyes.

I stood by Dad looking into the casket: Burton's face looked waxen and without the ever-present smile. It was the first time I had seen him in a suit. Dad turned to me.

"Since you are practically my law partner I don't feel that I am breaking the confidentiality code when I tell you that Peter is going to be the new co-owner and operator of Hickory Point Resort."

"Good for him," I whispered back. "Does Uncle Daryl know? It's rather ironic, don't you think?"

I located Junior, Joe, Jake, and Peter standing near the door waiting to perform their duties as pallbearers and motioned them forward. We stood together as I laid a small bouquet of flowers in the side of the casket. At the florist's shop they had attached silver letters to a silk banner that read, "For Uncle Burton from the BBs." The BBs executed a crude group hug and tried to hide tears from each other. When the funeral director approached to close the lid for the final time, I put my hand over Uncle Burton's and whispered silently, "Goodbye, my favorite uncle." The bouquet remained in the casket with Uncle Burton and the lid was fastened.

Winter trails

They come at night when I'm asleep
And leave their prints to let me know,
They came so near on freshened snow,
Their spoor-marked trails pass by my door:
Deer on the hoof, ermine that wore
Their winter coats, not meant to keep
When sunlight's strong and streams run deep.

They come in summer, I know that well,
But forgiving grass shows not a sign,
And they disappear into the pine
As if they hadn't paid a call
Or grazed beside the kitchen wall.
Who knows their journeys? Who can tell
When life was good? When darkness fell?

My winter's here, and there to view
Are all the trails I've made in life
As daughter, sister, mother, wife.
The twisting, turning, stopping gait,
The steps I took to shape my fate.

When spring returns and winter's through,
Let someone come to walk anew.

The lupine

Poets do bespeak the rose
In fable, verse and song.
Its beauty is immortalized,
And who's to say they're wrong?

But I prefer a lowly bloom
That needs no cultivation.
It grows in fields and multiplies
Without much adulation.

Their purple spires resist the frost
And wind, tho still adorn
The grandest hearth or quiet grave,
Yet never bear a thorn.

A home for William

Way back in the 1940s a psychologist named Maslow came up with a neat, triangle-shaped visual called *Maslow's Hierarchy of Needs.* It was explained in a lot of vague but impressive words like physiological, self-actualization, and hierarchy; but basically it said that not until humans are sheltered, fed and warm do they begin to think about relationships, love, music, art, and so on.

Heck! I already knew that from going on my Girl Scout camping trips. I knew from experience that you had to set up the tent, gather wood for a fire, and cook and eat that plate of beans and a char-roasted hotdog. Then and only then did you break out the guitar and sing fifteen verses of Kumbaya around the campfire. Oversimplification, you say? Why not?

Anyway, I might change that bottom block of Maslow's triangle to represent shelter alone, because nothing is going to happen, not even food, until you can get out of the weather or hide from danger. From the beginning of recorded time, humans – all life forms really – are initially obsessed with finding shelter from weather or danger: a cave, nest, log to hide behind or rock to crawl under. Modern man, I suspect at the urging of female partners, has throughout the ages refined that shelter obsession from cave to sod houses; bark to log lodges; then to bigger, finer homes and so on. Our children observe all this at a very early age. After all, they already know well the story of *The Three Little Pigs* and their struggle to find adequate housing.

Little girls often bypass eons of usable, if primitive, housing ideas to cut right to the chase: a doll house patterned after the very best of current homes. Theirs will have two floors, staircases, and patio doors.

So, what of our young sons who seem to have an inherent need to wrestle, tackle, and compete? What do our combative young men prefer in the line of shelter? You guessed it. Forts! Snow forts, tree forts, ditch forts. A fort can be made anywhere or of anything as long as it provides a certain amount of protection from attack and has open spaces for hurling missiles. My favorite fort story concerns my young friend, William, who overcame much adversity and disappointment to have the fort of his dreams, if only for a limited time. But then, dreams never do last long, do they?

Fort Menard

Doyle pulled the lid tab on a paper cup of McDonald's coffee and handed it to his partner, Anderson, who was driving the squad car. It was a sleepy, Saturday morning about nine a.m. in West Duluth, and the two police officers were making a routine drive around the business district doing a pre-opening, back-entry check of several stores. They had just rounded the side of the building into the front parking lot of Menards Home Supplies when Anderson spoke, "What's going on here?" Doyle was busy laying out a napkin and sweet roll on the dashboard but came alert when Anderson pulled the squad to a stop. Four or five boys, about eleven or twelve, were clustered on the sidewalk in front of Menards trying the doors and making frames of their hands on the glass to better see into the interior of the store. As the policemen got out of the car the boys whispered to each other, and then turned to face them. They didn't seem alarmed or frightened, just wary.

"You boys need some help?"

"We thought Menards opened early."

"Not until ten. You guys here to pick up something?"

"Naw, we just want to look around," the tallest said. Then the smallest pushed his way to the front and looked up at Doyle. His eyes were magnified by large, thick glasses which he pushed up his nose in the classic, knuckle maneuver.

"We came to see Willie's fort," he announced proudly. Several nearby companions nudged him in another classic maneuver which meant, "shut up."

"What?" he countered but was pushed to the back of the small gathering.

"What fort would that be?" Doyle was already starting back to the squad, but Anderson still seemed interested.

"We thought we might build a fort and came to see if we could get some ideas." The tall spokesman nodded and smiled at his companions, and they, a little too quickly, nodded and smiled together.

"Yeah, that's it."

"Sure, ideas.."

"Well, the store won't be open for another forty-five minutes, so you'd better move on and come back later."

They all ran off across the parking lot as Anderson got back behind the wheel.

"Something smells fishy here. We'd better check back later."

"What? You're thinking a major heist?" Doyle laughed around his sweet roll.

"No, but they may be planning on some shop lifting. When do little boys go anywhere for ideas? They just throw together a fort, if they're going to."

The day wore on with no major or minor crime to report in West Duluth. Around ten-thirty Officer Anderson parked the squad in front of Menards and both policemen strolled through the front door – no hurry, just a casual walk up and down the aisles, occasionally stopping to examine a tool or hold up a piece of plumbing like two cops on their breaks doing a little shopping while they were in the neighborhood. Then as they rounded into a snack aisle, Doyle touched Anderson's arm,

"Isn't that the little one with the glasses?" They spotted him just as he lifted a blister-wrapped package of beef jerky off the shelf and they walked over to stand in front of him. He looked up at the two, tall men, and his glasses rolled back toward his eyes unaided. All bravado was gone, and he turned a little pale.

"I was going to pay for this," he stuttered, "I've got the money." He rustled coins in his pocket and spilled a couple dimes on the floor. Anderson stooped to retrieve them and handed them back.

"See that you do," he said, "By the way, where's the rest of your gang?"

"They're around somewhere." Now he was nervous and hastily replaced the jerky on the shelf in a quick decision not to buy.

"Where's somewhere?"

"Somewhere in the back."

"Why don't you show us." The poor kid was visibly nervous now and looked as if each step was agony as he blazed a stumbling trail around lawnmowers and snow blowers, past the on-sale Christmas decorations, and into the back of the building where deep in the innards was a vast area obviously used for storing stacks of lumber, siding, trim, and so on.

The bustle of the store with its dozens of shoppers was left so far behind and so well insulated by tall stacks of cardboard boxes and piles of lumber that gradually the only sounds were the footsteps of the three who made up the short parade. Soon all that was visible were the ends of nine-foot-tall shelves of stored two-by-fours placed horizontally to the aisles. It was eerie. Their footsteps echoed off the ceiling. Somewhere in the guts of the building pipes clanked with inner distress. Occasionally the lumber itself made grating sounds, as if stretching under the strain of being piled so high.

Then, in the distance ahead, they heard laughter and voices, and turning a final corner they came upon a strange scene. Amidst all the floor to ceiling storage stood what appeared to be a perfect little one-room house. The fourth, front wall was absent, like a doll house design, but the space had been cordoned off by two lengths of pre-assembled picket fence, complete with gate, behind which two artificial fica trees bloomed attractively.

The room occupied the space made by about a nine foot gap in the shelving which formed the two side walls of the room. About six feet back could be seen the ends of stacked lumber in the next row to the rear, forming the back wall.

Two-by-fours had been placed across the top of the wall/ shelves to form a roof, and rugs covered the cement floor, one an artificial oriental which Doyle, distractedly musing to himself, thought would look nice in his living room. Patio furniture completed the comfortable looking abode. A fall theme wreath dangled from the end of one two-by-four on the back wall, its banner ribbon proudly proclaiming, "Home Sweet Home." The accidental gap in storage had produced a natural room or, as seen through the eyes of any twelve-year-old boy, a fort.

The designers sat inside on lawn chairs. Their backpacks were open on the floor in front of them, and they had evidently been interrupted at their lunch by unexpected guests, for plastic wrapped sandwiches lay open in their laps. When they saw the policemen, they stood, holding their sandwiches awkwardly. One boy was a good foot taller than the other, and the discrepancy in height seemed humorous to Doyle, as extremes often do. He couldn't hide a smile as he asked,

"What's goin' on, boys?"

"We're just playing. We didn't steal anything. We can put it all back."

"And you would be?"

"William,"

"Joe," chimed in the shorter one.

"Does anyone from Menards know you're back here?"

"Guess not." They both shook their heads and shifted nervously, looking at their feet.

"Did you have permission to play back here?" This question was answered by another head shake. "No," they answered in unison.

"Think we ought to take 'em in?" Doyle consulted his partner in too loud a voice, considering Anderson was right beside him.

"Let's see what Menards says. I'll go get someone."

The gang of boys had remained fixed by the encounter but now started shifting around and talking.

"We didn't do nothin."

"We just came to see Willie's fort."

"We've never been here before." Doyle decided to simplify the whole matter.

"Okay you guys, beat it! You two stay here." He motioned to William and Joe. The friends flashed a hasty, embarrassed glance at their unlucky friends and ran off in an unorganized retreat.

When Menard's manager arrived on the scene he was amazed and not amused. He picked up the end of a rug.

"Look at this. Now it's used goods. And all this patio furniture will have to be discounted. This is going to add up fast." He looked frantically around Fort Menard, and his eyes blinked rapidly like the windows of the digital cash registers in the check-out lines as they flashed a value for each item that crossed the counter.

William

William's mother remembered him as an exceptionally good baby, sleeping and eating on schedule and smiling up at her when she approached his crib. She took to calling him Sweet William after the flower that flourishes in shade and continued to call him that until he had grown to an age when his peers singled out his baby name for teasing. Even after the 'sweet' was abandoned, sometimes when she came home late from work and found her now half-grown son asleep, she would touch his cheek and whisper, "Good night Sweet William." William often heard the softly murmured wish but didn't dare respond lest he awake and spoil a dream.

William was a quiet, reserved kid, mostly because his older brother made all the noise and demanded all the attention. "Where's your brother? What did your brother do? Who was with your brother?" The questions were asked so early in his life and so often that he adopted a stock answer,

"I don't want to talk about it," and he stuck to it no matter who was doing the asking. Maybe now William has many dreams, ideas, and opinions worth hearing but just can't get past that rigid rule of his, or maybe no one has ever asked.

Jules, Eddie, Dan and Little Joe had been William's neighborhood friends since they were together in daycare. They played on the school ground, participated in after-school programs, and attended each other's birthday parties. They were surprisingly alike in many ways. Most of them came from broken homes, had learned for various reasons to keep their thoughts to themselves, and had little interest in school. Because they were always together, teachers and other authority figures tended to classify them as "a gang" and often undeservedly thought of them as displaying certain undesirable gang characteristics.

The truth was they were typical little boys; or maybe they were like typical little boys used to be before the age of video games and DVDs. They still hiked and rode their bikes in the summer and went sliding on Duluth's steep hills in the winter. They played neighborhood night games after dark: kick the can or hide and seek.

They loved playing football and even played for Irving Park, West Duluth. At first they lost; then Eddie's Dad (and Willie's mentor) started showing up at the games and led by William and Little Joe, they practiced, decided to be a team and started winning. They had high hopes for school sports, but in the fall were informed even before school started, that their grades weren't high enough to participate in extracurricular activities. They would have to wait a semester to see if they improved. By then the football season would be over. The boys abandoned the challenge during the first few weeks and settled for vacant lot football. Their organized sports participation slipped through the cracks of disappointment before they or anyone else even noticed.

As for building forts, that was still possible, but like animals that become endangered when their habitat is destroyed, urban sprawl seemed determined to thwart the gang's sheltering instinct. A tree in the neighbor's back alley made a wonderful lookout for approaching enemies and for raining down water balloons or ripe tomatoes. Then the boys looked on sadly as one day they watched men with chain saws made short work of the trunk with its planes and rough bark that had once made it easily climbed. They winced as the heavy branches that had provided rest and concealment dropped heavily to the ground. All this in order to make room for a new garage.

An abandoned gas station littered with empty metal barrels and old tires provided hours of play as they used basic architectural principles they didn't even know they had to stack walls and arrange hallways. This imaginative and extensive structure succumbed to the backhoe when the space was needed for a laundromat.

Even their snow forts, temporary from the onset, seemed to have to be abandoned early when a January thaw rendered them uninhabitable or a cross neighbor complained that, "There are too many kids hanging around here."

So the boys were restless and unconsciously on the lookout for a new fort site when a Menards happened to open in West Duluth. As fate would have it, not long after its opening, William and Little Joe visited the store for a look around, wandered into the back, and William's imagination took over with Little Joe as a dutiful accomplice.

Finding Yourself Not Quite Plumb

"Have you ever done something, then wished you could undo it?" Anderson was talking privately to Doyle as they stood to the side listening to Menard's manager berate the two boys.

"Do you two have anything to say for yourselves?" Of course, they didn't.

"Can't talk? Are you dumb? You must be to pull a stunt like this. This is not your property. It's stealing!" William spoke up quietly at this.

"We didn't take it out of the store. We didn't steal it."

"Oh, it does talk. Well Mr. Lawyer, we'll see about that. Maybe we'll call it vandalism. Anyway, your parents are going to have to pay for all this." He spread his arms wide encompassing the fort and several feet on either side.

William had a fleeting mind's eye view of his mother's face when she had to deny the boys something they thought they needed, and her voice was like an echo in his head,

"We can't afford it!"

"We'll put it all back. We'll clean everything up. We didn't hurt anything. We've only been here a couple days." Both boys were talking now, but their responses seemed to inflame the manager more than their silence.

"You won't touch any of this. You'll remember this little mistake. I'm pressing charges." Several Menard employees had gathered out of curiosity, and he turned to them. "Don't just stand there. Put this stuff where it belongs and then get back to work." He was almost screaming now, and both cops stepped forward to calm him down. Doyle motioned the boys off to the side. Anderson steered the manager down the aisle a few feet as if to speak privately.

"I don't think these boys meant any harm. They're just kids. They weren't thinking."

"That's the trouble with kids nowadays. They don't think. And their parents baby them, and you guys slap their wrists when they commit crimes. I want them charged."

"What do you want to charge them with?"

"Stealing!"

"They didn't steal anything. I don't say they shouldn't be punished, but they're already plenty scared."

"They took stuff off the shelves and moved it around."

"Isn't that what all your customers do?"

"This was different and you know it! They're gonna have to pay for all this stuff!"

"If they pay for it, they'll get to keep it. They'll have bought it."

"Oh no, I'll make a list of all this stuff." He turned to gesture towards the fort only to find that while he wasn't looking his minions had done as he had told them and carried off all the furnishings to the various departments all over the store. He hung his head in utter frustration and cursed under his breath.

It took a long time to sort it all out and much cajoling on the part of Anderson and Doyle; but in the end, William and Joe were taken home to their parents and told that they would pick up trash around the outside of the store for a month. Under no circumstances were they ever allowed in the store again.

When You Wish...

For several weeks Doyle and Anderson made a point of cruising Menards' grounds, checking to see if the trash was being collected. Occasionally they'd see the boys and stop to talk, but both of them remained quiet and guarded. One day, the cops went in the store to shop during their break. Anderson showed up in the check out line with several cans of paint and brushes, etc. He watched with a wry grin as

Doyle unloaded his cart. Sticking out of the back, rolled-up but recognizable, was the fake Oriental rug from Fort Menard and hanging on the cart handle, so as not to get crushed, was the "Home Sweet Home" wreath. Doyle caught his eye and pointed to the two items mouthing silently, "Not discounted."

Anderson laughed and then started thinking over the events of Fort Menard. When they had loaded their purchases and were pulling out of the parking lot he thought out loud.

"You know what those kids made wasn't really a fort."

"What do you mean?"

"It was too nice, and there wasn't anything you could hide behind and throw stuff."

"I know," Doyle nodded as if he'd thought the same all along, "It was more like a place they wished they had... a home.

"Damn, that was a clever idea though," Doyle nodded, and they shook their heads and smiled. "I wish," but the rest of his thought remained unsaid.

To my knowledge, William grew up without ever making another fort. It seemed to his mother that the episode wrenched him out of his childhood and deposited him in his turbulent teenage years before his time. I wish that he'd had a father who, among other fatherly duties, had taught him how to build and design, and to work with his hands. I wish his mother hadn't had to work so hard and long to support the family.

I wish that Menards had punished him by making him work in the store where he could learn about tools, and lumber, and building. Wouldn't it have been wonderful if they had taught him to build a real fort right there in the store and then offered classes for dads and their sons or daughters using their design and their materials? I know, I know, they're a business not babysitters or teachers.

I wish William and his mother could have known that for years the clerks who had been at Menards longest told their junior counterparts about the kids who built a fort in the store, and then I wish they had seen how they all laughed and shook their heads at the story. Of course clerks shared the story with carpenters who came to buy materials, and the cops alerted their colleagues and friends.

I wish that William and his mother knew that to this day the tale of William and Little Joe and the fort that was really a home is told by Duluth carpenters around their morning coffee. I just wish...

PROLOGUE TO
End of the Lupine Season

One sorrow never comes but brings an heir.

Pericles by Shakespeare

Note: This excerpt from End of the Lupine Season *– a full-length novel – centers on Madeline Island in Lake Superior near Bayfield, Wisconsin. Madeline Island is known by the Ojibwe as Moningwunakauning: "home of the yellow breasted woodpecker." The French established a fort and trading post (La Pointe) in 1693. Namesake Madeline was the Ojibwe wife of Michel Cadotte, chief fur trader there at the beginning of the nineteenth century. Scandinavian immigrants followed in the fishing and lumber trades. Since the mid 1800s, the Island has been a summer haven for tourists.* End of the Lupine Season *begins in the 1950s.*

 The moon was full, but even so it was a black night as the wind gusted and sent clouds scudding across the sky to cause sudden and frequent eclipses. Strangely, the gale hadn't produced rhythmic waves, but rather the surf seemed a confused boil responding not so much to the wind as to unknown forces beneath its surface.

Two Island policemen walked the beach with flashlights and tapes, cordoning off an area from the foot of the cliff descending stairs to the woods on either side of the beach and back to the shore, the lake itself providing the fourth side of a rectangle. Men arrived to offer help or to look; others, men and women, lined the edge of the cliff some 100 feet above to stand motionless, the squad cars parked behind them capturing their shapes with spinning lights and silhouetting an eerie, ghost-like audience.

The object of attention was a person sprawled in the sand about ten feet from the last stair. It was hard to identify it as a person; no human form was discernible. It looked more like a shirt and jeans carelessly cast aside by some impetuous swimmer in a hurry to take an impulsive midnight dip in Lake Superior. A woman and a man struggled down the stairs with a folded stretcher and rushed to kneel by the body.

"You can't do this one any good," one of the policemen said. "You'd best see if you can take care of Gudrun over there." He pointed to a middle-aged woman slumped in the sand. Her gray hair was blown wild in the wind, and she held her arms clasped tightly around her body, her hands on opposite shoulders in what was more like a lover's embrace than the usual tightly folded arms denoting withdrawal or protection. She stared straight ahead and rocked back and forth slightly. "I think she's in shock," the policeman said as he returned to measuring distances from stairs to body, from body to shoreline, and from body to woods, all of which he was carefully recording in a small notebook.

"You okay, Gudrun? Are you hurt? What happened? Where does it hurt?" There were no responses, and they settled for laying a blanket across her shoulders and trying to convince her to stand. But Gudrun had mentally retreated from the grim scene into her fantasy world, which would keep reality at bay until she could absorb what had happened. She was unwilling or physically incapable of answering questions, explaining events or even getting to her feet.

"Keep everybody off the beach. We don't want every yahoo and his maiden aunt down here stirring up this sand." Officer Nelson was uncharacteristically upset to the point of lashing out angrily at anyone who came near him. He struggled inwardly to remember and follow the proper procedures he had learned, years ago now, at a week-long law enforcement workshop. Procedures he hadn't been called upon to use until now. "Don't come down those stairs," he barked at a quickly descending figure.

"Hey Arvid, it's me!" A short, chunky woman entered the circle of his flashlight beam. "What happened? Does Gudrun need me?" He recognized Willow Peterson, Gudrun's friend, and immediately directed a path of light across the sand to where Gudrun sat rocking.

"Hey, honey it's me. What have we gotten into now? Come on up to the cottage. I'll make us some tea."

She looked at Arvid Nelson for approval, and he just nodded and once again shone the light to the stairs for them. Gudrun seemed to sigh in relief at the sight of her friend, and released her self-embrace as she maneuvered to stand, almost fell into Willow's outstretched arms, and leaned heavily as the two slowly made their way up the steep stairway.

Nelson paused for a moment to follow their ascent, shaking his head. He'd known Gudrun ever since she first came to the Island and started keeping house for the Gendrons, and he liked her. He'd often stop for a visit at the Gendron house on his rounds, and she always had fresh coffee and some of that Swedish baking she was so famous for with the summer people. "She's had a tough life," he mused "why do these things happen to good people? She was always so damn quiet, though, almost as if nothing ever touched her, kinda cold in a way." He shook his head again and returned to pace the beach, his eyes following the scanning trajectory of his flashlight.

The one room cabin was warm to the point of being stuffy, but Gudrun shivered with shock and her teeth chattered. She sat at the kitchen table, the blanket still draped across her shoulders. Her arms now lay across the oil-clothed surface, the palms of her hands turned upwards, almost in supplication. "What have I done?" she whispered. Willow saw her friend's face in agony as she turned from the teakettle in response to Gudrun's voice.

"You haven't done nothin'! Now don't be saying that! Who fell?" Willow's immediate response was to defend her friend. "Who's down on the beach?" Gudrun raised her eyes in surprise, having assumed everyone knew.

"It's LuAnn, Willow, our baby is dead, and it's my fault. I killed her." The last was but whispered. Willow reacted as if she'd been struck across the face.

"Nooo," she wailed. "What do you mean you killed her? Did you push her? Did you push her on purpose?" Willow was hysterical, but the questions went unanswered as Gudrun sank onto a chair and cradled her head in her folded arms on the table. Arne walked in at this point to view the two women silent and frozen in a momentary tableau of horror.

"No, she didn't push her! It was a terrible accident. The railing came loose," Arne explained.

"You can't be saying you did it then." Willow was immediately coherent. "People remember the first things you say when there's trouble, and you're in no shape to be answering questions."

"She leaned against the railing, it gave 'way, she fell," Gudrun had raised her head from the table, crying uncontrollably now and shaking with shock. Willow threw her body over the back of her friend holding her in her arms, and they rocked each other for a long time until the initial outpouring of grief had subsided.

"We have to talk this out, and get our stories straight, and you're in no shape to do that right now. Best you just keep quiet. Do you understand me?"

Gudrun nodded and let her eyes drop. One finger traced the outline of a flower on the tablecloth and as if having been granted permission, Gudrun again lapsed into her fantasy world where she had spent so many hours of her life. But a new and exciting story didn't reveal itself across the private screen of her mind. Instead, she found herself returning to the day she had first come to the Island at the age of 20. A day she often referred to as, "the day my life began."

The full novel, End of the Lupine Season, *will be published in 2012.*

About the author

Laurie Otis raised four daughters while following her husband's teaching career through several moves throughout Minnesota, Wisconsin, and Canada. She earned a B.A. with an English major from Northland College in 1973 and did advanced work in Library Science at the Universities of Wisconsin and Minnesota. Laurie worked for over 30 years as a librarian for Wisconsin Indianhead Technical College, Ashland campus, and later as a communications instructor and public relations representative. Retiring to her country home in Wisconsin, she enjoys writing, gardening, reading, pastel painting and yoga.

A major influence in recent years has been an affiliation with Washburn, Wisconsin's Stagenorth Theater. In addition to working as a stage manager and also with lighting and sound, she has had major roles in several plays: *Last Lists of My Mad Mother; Old Ladies Guide to Survival; Song of Survival; A Christmas Memory,* and *Moon Over Buffalo.*

Laurie took a First Prize at the 2012 Stagenorth *Writers Read* event, *Around the Table,* for her story *Life and Times at the IGA.*

To obtain her first novel, *The Amarantha Stories,* inquire at www.littlebigbay.com. An upcoming novel, *End of The Lupine Season,* will be published in 2012 and available at amazon.com.

ABOUT THE ILLUSTRATOR

Jan MacFarlane, whose illustrations grace these pages, graduated from the University of Minnesota with a degree in design. Her professional life always included some aspect of art: kitchen planning; merchandise display; calligraphy; and costume design for theater. She has also pursued icon painting and botanical art. Now retired, she works in pastel painting, metal jewelry smithing and drawing.

CPSIA information can be obtained at www.ICGtesting.com
Printed in the USA
LVOW111041210512

282607LV00003B/1/P